Bella donna

John Schertzer

SPUYTEN DUYVIL
New York City

ISBN 978-1-956005-39-4

Library of Congress Cataloging-in-Publication Data

Names: Schertzer, John, author.
Title: Bellamonia / John Schertzer.
Description: New York City : Spuyten Duyvil, [2022] |
Identifiers: LCCN 2021056036 | ISBN 9781956005394 (paperback)
Subjects: LCSH: Identity (Psychology)--Fiction. | Manhattan (New York,
  N.Y.)--Fiction. | LCGFT: Psychological fiction. | Satirical literature.
  | Novels.
Classification: LCC PS3619.C3497 B43 2022 | DDC 813/.6--dc23/eng/20211116
LC record available at https://lccn.loc.gov/2021056036

1

Downtown Manhattan, March 1988

He woke up in the living room, facing a scratch on the wall. His knees were separated at the joint and some of his toes scattered over the floor. Something stank. It wasn't puke or anything, just bad sweat, smelling like a filthy bar rag. He pushed himself up on his elbow, saw the halo of dampness beneath his body, and dropped himself back down. The clock's LED blinked twelve noon, as it probably had for the last several hours. He bounced up and ran to the bedroom. Bank receipts, envelopes, and coins went flying as he rummaged for the travel clock. Nine-forty. He saw it for a moment before it went blank, as the battery flew out of the back. That would make it about nine-twenty-three. Skipping a few steps on the way to the bathroom, he grabbed a photo of Sally that was stuck to his toe.

In the mirror his eyes swelled. His hair stood in a thicket of overgrowth. He splashed hot water on his face and lathered it, grabbed a disposable razor and only cut himself three times. His bloody gums turned the toothpaste pink. Reaching behind the curtain, he turned on the shower and adjusted the temperature before stripping. Letting out a long and emphatic flatus he stepped into the tub.

"Riiiinnng...," went the phone.

Grabbing a towel, slipping on the floor, he steadied himself and dripped back into the living room.

"Hello. Yeah, I'll be right in. No, don't let them go without me. I'm out the door. I'll grab a cab."

Slam!

Sally stood next to the soap dish. As he stood drying himself, he fought off a distracting urge spawned by the fear of impending doom.

His hair was wet and it was cold out, but it helped him wake up. A swarm of yellow cabs passed before he got to the corner, but by the time he arrived there was nothing. His jaw locked and his shoulders rode up around his ears. There was an empty one about three blocks down the avenue waiting for the light to turn. A woman beside him in a leather coat and tights held up her hand. He felt an inclination to hurl himself between her and the car, but turned away and let her take the ride, peeping down at the pathetic brown wing tips, draped by the gray that fell from his tattered black raincoat. He shamefully tucked his copy of *Amour Fou* into his coat sleeve and turned his twisted face away from the avenue.

As tension turned another notch, the neighborhood zoomed back, as if pressed tightly against a lens bulging outward from where he was standing. On the edge moved a cab with its roof light on. He held up his hand, and when it pulled up beside him, threw himself in.

"William and Fulton," he rasped, "just below the Brooklyn Bridge, two blocks east of Broadway."

The cabby was grayish, several days unshaved, with a frizzed ponytail. He fiddled with something on his lap and stuck it behind the visor, saying "Jeez, what a strange morning. You're like the third fare I picked up, and it seems like I've been out for hours."

"Oh yeah, slow?" Peter asked, pushing himself into the corner to get as much of himself out of mirror view as possible.

"Menacing. Frightening. Just look around. Some real baddies out there."

Peter looked out the window. He didn't notice. Beyond his own immediate terror, nothing seemed any more frightening than it ever was. "Sure, I see what you mean, man."

"I knew you would. I could tell the way you scrunched your head between your shoulders and rocked back and forth. Like you had to pee. Do you have to pee?"

Peter turned his attention to his bladder just to see if the lunatic was reading his mind. "No. Not yet."

"Yeah, see?"

Peter glanced at his watch. He didn't have a watch. He had lost it over a month ago, and didn't see the point in getting another one, not with all the clocks in the city. It didn't matter anyway. Late was late, though at this point life offered him a huge flexibility, one of the perks, he guessed, of this recent disintegration of credibility.

"Are you *the searcher*?" asked the cabby. He scratched his gray head and looked again into the mirror.

"Huh?" said Peter, startled out of his daze. The driver didn't repeat himself for a few moments, but when he did Peter realized he had heard right.

"Ah, what do you mean by 'searcher,' and what do you mean by 'the?'"

"Nothing. Just someone I was supposed to meet. I thought you might be him."

"Me? Isn't that some John Wayne western?"

"Something else, what *I'm* talking about. A card reader lady told me. You understand. I know it's a little weird. People think, too many tabs of acid," said the driver, tapping the side of his head, "maybe, waiting to get shipped off to Vietnam. Stuff like that. Sometimes I think it's TV that does it."

"I understand." Peter did. "I stopped watching."

"Christ! How'd ya do it?"

After avoiding television, movies, radio, and most magazines, for several months Peter was still suffering from heavy withdrawal symptoms and had trouble picturing himself without the image getting overlaid by that of a cop, rock singer, or a standup comic. This happened particularly during times of duress or fatigue, and especially while trying to *visualize* his way out of an unpleasant situation, say, when he found himself trying to explain himself to people, most frequently his boss or Sally. He hoped that something of his real self might eventually emerge if he flushed the system, something besides a willowy emptiness, a turbulent nothing, if there was, in fact, anything else.

But there was something else, something more disturbing, and that was the thing he didn't like to think about.

"I turned the damn thing in," he said. "Gave it to Good Will."

"Drastic measure."

"Takes determination."

Ten minutes later he was in the elevator drilling a fingernail into the seam of his coat pocket. He got off at the 14th floor and tried to sneak past the receptionist.

"Peter, good afternoon," said sweetly smug Marion, looking and sounding like Mother Theresa's fashion model grand niece. "Dave would like to see you first thing."

He grabbed the message she was holding out to him, a radiant fuchsia-pink paper rectangle inscribed, in perfect penmanship, with Sally's name and other crucial details. The time, checked off, was 9:15 AM. He stuffed it in his shirt pocket and rushed to his cubicle, removed his coat, brushed himself off, felt himself sweat for a few moments, and walked over to Dave's office. Dave's secretary was away from her desk, so he knocked on the door. It opened with a grave swing, slowly revealing the blue vested, red tied figure.

"Hi Dave."

Dave stood, looked at him blankly, eyes slowly sharpening, individual hairs rising electrically out of his auburn dome. He wore a look that struck Peter on the chest and sent him backwards a few millimeters. Eyes locked, they wrestled for a moment, and Peter felt himself diffuse into the atmosphere of the room, shocked into attentiveness. Dave looked away, went back to his desk, sat.

"The other day I saw a woman with feet so swollen she could hardly balance unless she held onto something," he said. "She was also missing some toes. You know I'm not a charitable guy but I gave her a few bucks because I don't need shit like that on my conscience when I've got an office to run. It makes me feel like a good guy, like I care, like I'm doing the best I can. A couple of weeks ago I ran into some clown whose skin looked like it was just about to fall off of him, and I gave him a five-spot just for the show." For a moment his head turned, his eyes giving Peter a disinterested stare. He turned back to the wall and continued. "Again—I'm not generally charitable, and I don't want you to confuse me with someone who is. I don't go handing out paychecks around here just out of the goodness of my heart, you know."

Peter behaved himself: sat and listened, as if taking in some new and important information.

"I like to run things pretty loosely around here," Dave continued, standing up again, pacing briefly as he kept his eyes on Peter, "as you can probably tell. I like it that way, and that's the way other people like it—I think." He looked away and walked to his chair and sat down, put his elbow on the desk and stared out of the window.

"Some people don't."

There was a pause. A silence of fifteen seconds. It spread itself throughout the office in a mist, making the air seem fresh and light, ready to yield, with traces of horror film glimmer seeping in from the edges.

"My boss, for instance, Mort Johnston, doesn't like it one bit. People like him would just love to shut us down, Pete. He could absorb our services into a whole lot of other areas he can more easily justify keeping alive. He's from the old school. Can't live with ambiguity. I think he even goes to church." Dave's head rolled back around, drawing Peter deeper into his trance. "I'd like to keep it, this little strange machine we've got going here. I worked hard to grow it into what it's become. But to them, it doesn't make sense. It shouldn't exist. Doesn't follow any textbook architecture of departmental design. More of an organically grown squiggly thing that drives them nuts every time I have to explain the accounting, and what we do here. You don't know the resistance I go up against almost every day. And every day I beat it. And sometimes your input helps a great deal.

"But I had that meeting with Schenk today—Schenk the ballbuster—and where the hell were you? I looked like an idiot in there. And you, snoring away at home with the bottle shoved up your ass. Don't tell me it was the plumbing again. That didn't work last month. It's late in the quarter, Pete. You know that."

"Yes sir."

Dave picked a cigarette out of his pocket and tapped it on his desk, then held it down on an angle until it bent. "I can't take another chance like this. I know you won't fuck up again. On another day it mightn't have made a bit of difference. You know I don't give a shit about time. You have it, when you need it. That's the way I want it for me, more rope to hang myself. And it's only fair."

Peter began wondering what was wrong, whether he was still drunk from the night before, or something more severe. What was this incandescent calm, so untypical of him, that he seemed to be bathing in—none of the usual panicking, sweating, the melee of paralyzing thoughts whirling through his head.

"Just don't fuck me up again or I'll let you have it."

With this, Dave's eyes radiated toxicity. His head changed size and shape minutely, but his eyes stayed locked in place. At this point Peter broke back into being his old self again, the percolation of his stomach, increased activity of his sweat glands, tightness of his limbs, facial musculature, surging of his blood, faintness near to tipping over.

When he got back to his desk, Peter yanked at the fuchsia note in his shirt pocket, tearing small sections off one by one until there was little left of it, feeling his hangover shift gears, scattering with the pink scraps raining down on his desk. He dropped his head in his hands, pressed his palms into his eyes, watching the geometric patterns forming over his closed eyelids. He tossed a stack of old papers in the trash, picked up the phone, and gingerly tapped out Sally's number.

"Verity Travel. How may I help you?" came a cheerfully bloodless voice.

"Yes. I want... Is Sally Cantor there?"

"Sure thing. Hold just a moment."

His fingers tapped twice and grabbed at his knee. On top of the computer monitor stood a picture of Sally, blonde and upright, with softness chiseled into severity. The glare of the Plexiglas frame was broken in the middle by a faint scratch, which fell across her chest like a palm, making her seem most generous and tolerant.

"Hello, this is Sally," said a voice he drank in that burned on the way down.

"Hi. You called?"

"Oh, it's you," she said. "I was worried. I thought you might have done yourself in. You know, after that..."

"Shit..." said Peter. "I know I keep promising. But things aren't that bad. I don't think." He listened eagerly for her reply.

"If they were you'd probably have me to blame."

"Not to blame. You'd be involved, surely, but there's no blame."

"I'm always involved, aren't I?" Sally asked.

"What do you mean?"

"Somewhere inside you're always blaming me for everything. I mean really, despite what you say."

"That's not true. I never gave you any reason to believe that. That's you, your guilt. I only said that when things are good with us nothing else seems to matter as much." He slouched and sketched invisibly on his desktop.

"So I'm at least the cause of your feeling the brunt of it, that mythic agony of yours. If I was more *considerate*, a servant only to your desires and expectations, you'd be happier. You think."

"Okay, okay, let's get off it. I don't feel like arguing. I feel like my whole life is an argument."

"Fine." He heard something between a grunt and an exhalation.

"But Peter," Sally continued.

"Yes?"

"What are you going to do if you lose your job?"

"No such luck."

"No, I'm serious. Think about what I'm saying! What? Are you going to move back with your parents or something?"

"*A*—I'm not going to lose my job over this. That's not how the story goes. *B*—Even if I did, I would be able to find another one. I'm not helpless, you know."

"Sometimes I wonder."

"Look, I'm here every day. I never call in sick, late sometimes, yes, but they're not getting rid of me over something like that."

"Don't be so sure."

"It's just that my brother, you know how he likes to live it up. It's not like he's in the city all the time, you know. He's like…"

"I know, Mr. Hyde, after finally killing Dr. Jekyll."

"No, no, no—not that. I used to think Rasputin, before he shaved his beard."

"Ha! He's nothing like Rasputin. Rasputin was intelligent, first of all, and he was a hell of a lot more charismatic than Dennis will ever be. He was kind of wise, a mournful schizo, maybe, you know, like that guy we met that time at *Moisture*."

"Oh, you mean that hippy hypocrite? The one who tried to read your palm? What was he, Eh-stone-ian? All those hippy eurotrash jerks are the same. Think they've got soul because they can rattle off a lot of fluff about dead German philosophers, like their spoiled-brat American, ivy-fed cousins, your friend Janet, as for instance. They're really all pretty two dimensional, despite all that metaphysical vomit they can hurl at you in every shape and stench."

"Oh, and you're not." She had often called him out for being a little too proud of growing up in a classic suburban neighborhood where more kids just happened to end up in prison than elite colleges.

"I don't know what I am. Fractured. I feel like a broken mirror, a wheel of surfaces. Depth is no option."

Sally spat laughter into the phone. "Yeah. Yeah. Almost right. More like a broken record. *Wheel of surfaces*, my ass. I'm going to have to stop lending you my books."

Peter rocked and then slouched in his chair.

"I hope you at least made him stay," said Sally.

"Oh, Dennis? Nah. But don't worry. One thing I can say about him, he's got a great automatic pilot."

"Make sure he wills it to you. You can have them remove it at the morgue some night."

"Forget it. There's more chance he'll get mine, but I don't see how it would do him any good."

"I'll say. Oh, and by the way, the reason I'm calling, my *brat* friend Janet can't do it any other night this week, so I'm getting together with her later. If you want to meet me for a little while, I can do it, but you'll have to come up here." He sank further into his chair. Janet hated him. He hated Janet. Though he had tried briefly to befriend her, she just wouldn't have it.

His stomach began to wrestle with itself. A small red light began flashing on his phone. He stammered and watched it blink, feeling it pulse in his temples. "Look," he said. "I've got another call coming in. I've got to take it."

"That place at Grand Central. You've got an hour, hour-and-a-half before she shows up."

They hung up, and so had the other line. A list gurgled up from his inner database:

Record 1 She think(who) she is?
Record 2 Doing.always this_to_me.
Record 3 Shefeel() Not= love-me.
Record 4 Do(care) not what says(she).
Record 5 Me -> just_a_toy & piss_me_off.
Record 6 How (long) I_going_to_take_it?

Record 7 Me -> Feel small.

Record 8 CanDo(1, "yo_tengo") -> nothing.

Record 9 I not(can) even_stand_up_for_myself.

Record 10 Me -> (perfect) slave.

Record 11 ***Why_do_I_let_her_do_this_to_me?

Record 12 Id_never_Get_away_with_Anything_Like_that.

Record 13 She.rights <- she->important.

Record 14 Im_not.

Record 15 Im_not_as_lovable_as_She_is.

Record 16 Im_Not_Beautiful.

Record 17 Im_Ugly_and_Despicable.

<<FATAL ERROR>> eof() = .t.

He let his head fall into the palm of his hand. He wore it like a patch over his left eye as his right blurred and fell on the stapler, daring it to transform, lose its banality. The cartridge shot out when he pressed the button on the back, spilling staples across the top of his desk. Composing himself, he eyed a small woven square of matches made like the rafts children make of popsicle sticks. He picked it up gently between his thumb and forefinger and inspected it like an archeologist would an object he was trying to catalog, disturbed by the precision and delicacy he had at certain mindless moments. Four bulbs flush against each side—cardboard sown into a kind of fabric. A chill traced through him as he realized he couldn't remember doing it, although he knew, and recognized his handy work. There was a small terror that had often accompanied Peter's hangovers, with the idea that he was losing his mind, or that his consciousness was getting sucked away from him. As his dread expanded and spread deeper into his body, he shook his fist at Sally's photo and swept his arm, dumping the staples and the stapler into the trash.

2

Up above were the constellations painted on the ceiling of Grand Central Station, and around them the ostentatious curlicues of Social Darwinism. He looked around trying to imagine himself a Morgan, a Vanderbilt, but couldn't straighten his plebe spine into anything but an awkward kink. What would it have felt like? It was easier to imagine being a dog. A dog sits up and listens, waits for a treat, foolishly runs off after a stick, or craps in the appropriate place. He tried to strut, to flourish, but then stiffened, noticing a panhandler stamping his feet and laughing at him. Peter turned to walk away, but stood for a moment, remembering.

Years before he had seen a gorgon of a woman pass that very spot. She must have been eight feet tall, with clubbed feet and a huge sausage nose, almost a trunk, and she had shocked him into an eerie sort of reverie. No one else had seemed to notice, but she was obviously there, in worn, but otherwise conventional commuter clothes. But how could such a being even exist, and not even be noticed by the surrounding crowd? It was when he was still young, and those kinds of things were only beginning to happen to him, occurrences that were still inexplicable, impossible, but had somehow begun to seem more ordinary over time. It used to panic him excessively. But it was also one of the reasons he decided to find work in New York, since part of him seemed to be drawn toward a life he didn't understand

and couldn't explain, and though the suburbs were good for their beaches and endless lawns, it was the crammed-in threat of a place like Manhattan where he could find images that matched his feeling for the world, being something monstrous and uncontainable, something you always miss by trying to identify it. For a moment he felt the memory flicker, tried to hold onto it, but it flashed away with a comic book rudeness, and was soon off scampering the halls of the station.

And of course, the other big reason was Sally. The city was her world, as she had grown up nearer to it, had more often inhabited its spaces, and could put it on like a second skin, move through it with grace and pleasure. She was, he suspected, in many ways a more advanced human being than he was, superior in so many ways, and that knowledge continually haunted him, as this inferiority made him feel unworthy of her attention and her love. And so he strove to adapt, to so dutifully become something he was not, at least not yet, but could perhaps, and this condensation of chaotic forces, its violence and infinite variations of worlds he could barely imagine, the many people and languages, the kaleidoscopic apocalypse of too many lives and ideas, where every other fucker was an artist, or pretended to be, could in some ways be a training ground or a maze he could run, and figure out, to broaden himself closer to her dimensions. One of the many ways he would do so was to familiarize himself further with the complex strangeness. If Sally could move about comfortably unconscious of the barbs and horrors, he would advance by absorbing every little nuance of them, attend to each minor detail and seek out whatever underlying pattern he could and diagram it in his mind, understand how he connects and ways he is more like oil in water, while Sally was much more a fish, heart and soul part of the substance that encases her, in which she navigates, gives her life and returns it in equal measure. In comparison, Peter was more a piece of gum stuck to a shoe, sticking to everything and producing all sorts of awkward movements in the body of whatever he had attached himself to.

Yet this whole sense of lack had also very often provoked in him a defensiveness, a jerky arrogance he tried to contain without success. And it was this that stabbed in those moments after-the-fact, when he had reflected on what just happened—how did a blow-up come about, and how did he find himself down some strange ever-looping and self-immolating corridor?

After a frenetic interrogation of every corner of the concourse, he found the place. He stuffed himself through the crowded doorway and huddled in his raincoat between the jukebox and the door, until a spot at the bar opened up. He wedged himself in between two other bodies and stared at the mahogany counter, working his jaw loose with his hand. It was an up-scaled dive, reified by the installation of chipboard walls, and a number of sandblasted Plexiglas panels trying to look like cut glass behind the bar. He sat drinking a scotch, grinding his teeth, imagining what he might tell the guy who redesigned the place, while the woman on his left continuously leaned back against him or jabbed him with her elbows every time she laughed. On his right was a man with a two-day beard, and slitted, moist eyes, who smiled and raised his glass as if trying to provoke conversation. Peter grabbed a pencil that somehow made it into his jacket pocket and tried, very unsuccessfully, to make wood grain tracings on a cocktail napkin, until remembering that there was a buffet in back during happy hour. He gave up his stool and pushed his way back.

The steaming serving tin gave off a sweet, not-quite-rotting odor of leftovers. He gripped his sweating scotch glass, and taking a biting slug, clapped it down on the corner of the tablecloth. Grabbing a hot hors d'oeurves plate he lifted the cover of the tin. Egg rolls and ziti sat side by side in two separate trays. He filled his plate with a little of both and began chumming it down, occasionally lifting his glass for a small dribble to dampen his mouth. He continued noisily on for some minutes, filling his plate twice again, until he felt a tug on his jacket. He turned around in irritation, his right elbow almost striking Sally's chest.

"Well, well," he said, trying to garble through a mouthful of mashed pasta.

"Been here long?" she asked.

"I've been here since before six. *Finally…*I stopped and had a drink. It's about time you showed up," he said as he wiped his mouth on a damp cocktail napkin.

She crossed her arms and smirked. "You jerk." She shifted her head and pointed with her chin. "I've got a table over there. I've been watching you make a pig of yourself."

"Bullshit."

"Uh huh."

"Yeah well, how long you been there?"

"Oh, about twenty minutes, probably."

"Bullshit. I haven't been here for twenty minutes."

"No. You just got here. I've been here that long."

He held his breath and followed her to her table. "Honestly," he said, "I checked back here." A waiter came and dropped a basket of bread sticks between them. Peter reached inside his jacket and threw a pack of cigarettes and a book of matches on the table, waited for a response, and then grabbed the pack and tore open the cellophane with all the brutality he could muster. Sally sat calmly back, wine glass in hand, without a sign she'd noticed. She always seemed to make him jump and he had no apparent effect on her whatsoever. He thought back to the flow charts he had tried to make of what he imagined of her inner-life — simple but varied drawings he had made on yellow legal pad, with felt-tipped pen — in hopes of discovering leverage points, but the fragile diagrams fell to pieces in his mind. There was a chattering of many voices through which a disco beat could be discerned. Into the cheerful bedlam, shards of his Sally-image confetti flocked the entirety of his awareness.

"So you won't go out with us tomorrow night," she said, looking away. "Is it that you don't like dancing anymore, or have you just grown out of clubbing?"

"I didn't say that. I just said I was a little short this week. I'd rather wait till next week. I don't see why we can't just stay home, you know, alone together." Peter flicked his swizzle stick against his front teeth.

"Will you stop that!" Sally grabbed it out of Peter's hand. "I hate it when you do stuff like that when I'm trying to talk to you."

"You're a wreck," he said. "You gotta learn to relax a little."

She laughed and shook her head. "I can't believe you." She took a sip from her wine glass, poised as if she were looking through him. "If you're always having trouble with money, well, why don't you do something about it, huh? Or do you just want to have a convenient excuse all your life?"

"No." Peter sat up and shifted, as if buckling a seat belt.

"I can't see why you don't get a roommate. I've been saying it all along. Your space is big enough. You just won't listen to me."

"I am. I mean, I'm working on it. I put up flyers."

"You're kidding, aren't you?"

Peter began flicking his teeth again, but Sally tolerated it. "No, I'm not. I actually got a call already, but only one, and I'm planning on putting more up tomorrow."

"Well?" Sally sat forward and shot her eyes into his.

"Some guy named Frank. Didn't sound like someone I'd want to live with."

"How's that?" She sat back again, grabbed Peter's cigarette pack and began tapping it against the table.

"He made me nervous; not a lot, but the way he sounded—I detected a pathology."

"You what?" She smacked the pack down hard, denting an edge. Peter took it calmly from her hand and leaned back, bringing together the fingertips of his splayed hands.

"I feel I intuited something I didn't like about him."

Sally's hand still stood suspended and curled, as if clutching something. "That's a lot to get from a message on your answering machine. So, what did he sound like?"

"He had a stutter."

"Oh, Peter."

"No, but it was a *mean* stutter. And it sounded purposeful, like he was mocking me."

"You don't stutter."

"Not outwardly, no."

"That's it—you've got to see a shrink or something."

"*I'm* working on myself." He poked his chest with his index finger. "Me! Me!"

"*Right*. You're working on my patience, more like it." Sally seemed to recede into a shadow. She tapped softly, her bracelet clicking rhythmically against the table. "Peter, why don't all the other people we know have problems like this, condescending phone messages from weirdo, would-be roommates? I don't know why I have to put up with this all the time."

"You don't. That's it. Maybe it would be different if you did."

"But I don't see it that way."

"Look, I had a hard day, all right? And I admit that maybe I'm a little hyper-sensitive, but I'm not making this up. The guy sounded rude, and a little crazy, besides."

"Well, that decides it; you two should get along just fine."

"Ahhh…" Peter dropped his head on the table, a little harder than planned, and then sat back up, rubbing his brow.

"Peter, if I were you I'd consider plugging the TV back in, tearing off that wretched drawing you taped over the screen, and read less of those creepy books you've been reading."

He looked at her sideways, mildly shocked.

"Really," she continued. "I might even come over more often if there was some entertainment around your place."

"Hmm...!" Peter lit a match and stared at it, resting his palm on his chin. "You just want me to be like everybody else."

"You're already like everybody else."

3

He heard the clunk of his boots as he walked down the sidewalk, carefully trying to avoid the place where he slipped on dog shit earlier. Half way down the block he realized he was headed the wrong way and turned back, stepping right into it. Under a nearby streetlight, he looked at the bottom of his boot and tried rubbing it clean in the dirt beneath a tree. He thought about going back and changing his shoes, but then continued on, after considering where he was going. As he rounded the corner the lights grew brighter and the traffic mounted. A white truck rumbled by, pouring thick black smoke into the air. It washed over Peter as he held his breath. With each reek he picked up he began to feel more himself. It was good to smell like diesel in the cold air, better than dog shit, at least. It reminded him of when the garbage trucks would come on winter days, when he was a squirt playing out in the snow. All the kids would stop and watch the monsters brush off the lids with worn leather gloves, breathing big clouds of frost. Peter would breathe with all his might, but his little lungs could only exhibit a cloud about a quarter of their size. Now he forced out a slow breath as he walked, but the steam scattered quickly in the breeze blowing out through Tompkins Square Park.

The park provided its own richly acrid scents, choking him as he passed through the paths lined with the homeless, squatters burning refuse they can set fire to for heat, paper, old tires, anything they could get their hands on, to stay alive and keep the others alive, the ones who couldn't help themselves, through the winter and these early days of spring. There were the matted-haired lunatics wrapped in layers of clothing, ill-fitted and worn over the wrong parts of their bodies, a tee-shirt over layers of pants, or wrapped around arms, as gloves, plastic bags tied to feet up to ankles to protect from the damp; teenage kids with Mohawks or hair wadded into large spikes, hennaed or made green or blue, faces covered with dirt, barely visible in the dark. Voices called for change, food, any sort of valuable, and some sources of those voices would push their way toward him, mildly or not so mildly threatening to take something if had something to give. But it was obvious that Peter, of all people, was not carrying anything worth getting violent about.

He was always relieved to exit the area, though he made it a practice to walk through whenever he could. A little part of him believed that he belonged there, that he was meant to suffer in some way other than the continuous panic brought about by a relationship always on the verge of disintegration, and a job, a wrong job for him to be working, one that he hated, and scared the shit out of him, but the only kind of job he seemed to be able to get, one in which he seemed barely competent. He didn't know what he wanted to do, but working in an office, a corporate cubicle job, was not it. It paid the bills, however, and a larger part of him was more frightened of living among the campers in the park, being constantly hungry, cold, beaten, raped, often not living past their twenties.

It was a long road that got him to feeling this way about himself. Friends who had therapy helped him figure that out – the angry and arguably alcoholic father and kids at school who'd often find him an easy target for their amusements, both body and mind. His family was perhaps a little bit more wealthy than the majority of these working-class kids, not much, but the fierceness of their resentment was felt in fist-falls and words that hurt even more to hear. Except for a few close friends, girls had shunned him because of the rumors they heard, the supposed disgusting and inhuman things he had done, none of which he could remember, though he had at times found himself waking up in a pool of vomit on some stranger's lawn.

Outside *The Source* was a throng of people being herded by wooden barricades. A man's head hung over his huge shoulders as he scanned I.D.'s with a penlight and waved them in one at a time. He didn't move a muscle save his arms, and his head sometimes when he'd raise it a half an inch and let it fall again. In front of Peter was a woman with bleached cellophane hair and the thin arms and legs of a junky. Her throat was pink and smooth, delicate and medieval, but her mouth was a deep blood red. She was with a man as thin and fragile as she was. Peter thought of himself and compared, as he looked through the mess in his wallet and dropped his driver's license on the ground. No need for so much meat, not around the midsection. In a sweeping motion he picked it up, scratching the edge against the concrete, holding it for the titan who paid no attention and let him pass. Inside he handed a girl at a podium five dollars and received an invisible stamp on his right hand, one of an eye in a triangle, an eye that looked much more like a gaping wound.

Dry mouthed and introverted, moving into the smoke and din, he passed a concession and bought a can of Bud. It was twice what he'd pay somewhere else, which was twice what he'd pay at a grocery, that being about twice what they paid, and how much did they pay the poor slobs in Milwaukee who made the stuff? He went on with his Pythagorean accounting until he decided it was okay because the bastards probably had lots of rent to pay, and who else was going to pay it if not other poor bastards like himself.

Almost peeling the paint off the walls with explosions and sounds like the warblings of truck-sized dolphins, the speakers barked an ear-numbing melee, coagulating and segmenting time in repetitive shapes, set on shutting down the mental processes and putting everyone at ease. Peter, who always had trouble finding the track switch between one mode of mood and another, strained his attention until the noise grew sensible. A voice sang, "Mama I wanchoo. Baby, I got your panty-urge." He was settling into the ebb and flow of sounds and bodies. The next tune, though it was hard to tell where one ended and the other began, was even more braided with barbed-wire cacophony. There were numerous instruments breaking in, squawking, and disappearing, while a number of voices said things he could neither hear nor make sense of, like a walk through a crowd of lunatics at a street fair bathing him in phantasms and vague recollections, exotic and obscene graffiti.

Gray smoke rose and filled his brain, eyes dulled and crossed as the watery forms of sound and movement laid claim to his body, penetrating with an absent-minded rock and sway. By the time he had become a mere object on the edge of the dance floor he responded to something tugging at a thread of his person, turning him around in a semi-circle. A pleasant panic registered, cued somehow by the information that had just begun to fill his visual field, until the form took shape and he was back again. The blood redirected itself into his face. Out of the cloud of erotic mayhem emerged the form of Sally's friend, Iris.

Around her face, the brown, least abstracted flesh he had noticed since he arrived, billowed a cloud of dark, electrically fried hair. From the middle, her mouth drew the rest of her features back invitingly, making the corner of his own mouth twitch. It occurred to him that he hadn't seen her for a while. But her smile began fading as he stood dumbly. He took this to mean that the others were very near, and so struggled to speak. But the words came out of her mouth much quicker than they could form in his own. His opened up just as she began telling him something and he missed it.

"Nothing," she said when he asked her. "I was just saying hello."

"Oh, hello then."

"Same old Peter. God, I missed you, and this is what I get." Her face wrenched in a half grin and turned to the side.

"Shit, I'm sorry Iris. It's just that I don't know what to say sometimes until somebody else starts off."

"Ho ho. I can remember you having plenty to say, usual-ly when you're drunk. Whatever. At least I got you talking. Now go on. Say how nice it is to see me."

"It is. It really is. How was your trip?"

"Great, but I'll tell you about it later. It's too noisy in here. Now, give me a hug."

They embraced and Iris planted a wet kiss on Peter's neck which made him shudder, almost driving him away.

The place was still sparsely populated, so it was easy enough to spot the others coming. There they were, the menacing blonde and her evil cohort, Janet, who stepped up without looking at him or saying a word. Sally moved in beside Peter and put her hand through his hair. "Now," she said, "that wasn't too long, was it?"

"No, but it was a beautiful walk down here. I think you would have enjoyed it," Peter said.

"There he goes again," said Iris.

Janet's jaw slung low as she shook her head. "It's fucking cold out," she said in a way that seemed almost friendly for her.

"He'd probably walk rather than take a bus if Manhattan was under attack," said Sally. She looked at him smirking.

Peter was flustered. "Who would ever attack Manhat-tan? Shoppers?" His eyes met Janet's and an uneasy trill made him look quickly away. He looked back, but she was already gone.

The predatorial club regulars were filtering in and seemed to gather around their little group, mainly boys-soon-to-be-men perhaps trying to score older women for self-enhancement and sexual credibility. Groups of them appeared to be theme-dressing: the black or gray shirts with single-tone variations of red-spectrum tie, the camouflage pants and under-sized tee shirt and crucifix, turtle-necked drones in mod hair and horn-rimmed glasses, the down-to-earth plaid flannels over waffle thermals and jeans. Peter, himself, may have fallen into a null category of cowboy boots, faded black khakis and limp, over-worn tee shirt. He generally tried to dress as banal as possible in order to deflect the wrong kind of attention (i.e. his own), but he wondered what he was doing with the particularly self-conscious, not to mention uncomfortable, foot-gear, though it was probably the single feather in his cap of hipness that sneaked through his self-critical filtering system. There were holes everywhere – in his shirt, pants, his attention span and his comprehension of his surroundings. You couldn't block every one of them, or else you'd be blocked, he'd tell himself, waiting for the next thing to tear, hoping it would at least be for the best, something trendy or enlightening.

Janet returned and passed out beers to Iris and Sally and began to scope out the uninvited swarm of testosteroids for a victim. Peter tipped his empty can and looked into the opening. An eyedropper's quantity of suds sloshed around the bottom. He tipped his head and felt it hit the back of his throat and crushed the can, giving the invaders a stern look, and was off to get himself another.

The woman at the concession ignored him while she served three people who had come after. Eventually he got his beer, but not without a mild confrontation. Looking over his shoulder he saw Sally flirting with a broad smile and bright eyes and turned away to explore a corridor. It was poorly lit but lead to a room whose brightness threw shadows back at him from the braces set into the walls. It was only a lounge area outside the piss rooms, furnished with automobile seats, tiled along their edges with small plastic toys, otherwise vacant except for a badly rendered mural of Dalí's *The Great Masturbator*, and a man approaching with a smile, wearing a thin moustache and short, gelled-back hair.

"Jonesy!" said the man, addressing Peter in an upper-crusty, British twang. "Jonesy, you evil bastard, how've you been?" He stepped up. Peter stood mute and embarrassed for a moment, as the other extended his hand athletically. Peter grasped it saying, "I'm sorry. I'm not who you think I am."

"Such crap!" said the man. "You do this to me every time, well, one time. Of course you are. You're that lad from Michigan with the brilliant Ecstasy. Right? Remember? How about a bit now? Either that or change the lights in this place, they're making me feel a little too present."

Peter's memory could be spotty, but not this spotty, and though there was evidence he might drift temporarily into fugue at moments of high intoxication, the man's story didn't fit with any of his collection of self-narratives, not even any of the most masochistically adventitious. But no matter what he said he couldn't convince the fellow, whose mouth seemed to function with far greater fluency than did his ears, and far more formidably than his own mouth and ears, and in fact far more than almost anything Peter had except perhaps his ability to panic.

Peter finally tried to bring the whole transaction to a halt with a, "Well, it was sure nice making your acquaintance, but I've got to get back to my people," which beaded up and fell away like a sweat droplet on the hood of a freshly waxed Jaguar XJ6. Peter honestly did find the man likable, mistaken identity and all. So instead of abandoning his companion, who called himself Lamont, he compromised by inviting him back to the group. Lamont declined, but followed him out anyway, and when Peter reached his party, stood at a few yards, squinting through a glassy aloofness.

When he rejoined the group, they all moved toward the stairs without a word said. Lamont followed a few steps behind, slit-eyes peeping out of his lowered head. Up above, in the dance hall, there were more people than below, but still plenty of room to move. Most of them swayed, careened and sweated as the volume of the music rose almost unnoticeably slow. Some stood shouting at each other and laughing. Peter noticed that the ceilings were very high and covered with big pieces of chipped paint in leafy patterns. At one end was a stage where perhaps cabarets had once been performed. A chic looking boy with an exquisitely torn tee-shirt and a tangle of chains sat on the edge drinking and surveying the crowd. His eyes met Peter's for an instant. Lifting a beer to his lips, he looked away. Peter watched him for a while trying to remember what it felt like being young and having the type of arrogance it took to hold that kind of composure. At twenty-seven, that central point on the slide down from twenty-five to thirty, all he could accomplish was the bumping of his mild dread into his soft wall of repugnance. As it caressed him and held him gasping inwardly, he compressed back to a point of senselessness. There was a music in him, or more a tone, that stretched and rose above all the peaks. It was his own inner voice telling him to quit, to go home. When the girls started dancing, he hardly noticed, though they took turns pecking at him and tugging on his shirtsleeve. Lamont stood facing him waiting like a butler a few yards away. Peter gazed at him and he approached. He stopped before Peter and put his hand to his mouth coughing as his eyes swept the floor.

"You know, you look menacing like that, just standing there," He shouted. "I wouldn't put it past someone to start something with you," he shouted.

"Why? What do I look like?" asked Peter.

"You look like a hooligan waiting to take what you think is owed you."

The side of Peter's mouth rose in a troubled grin, his eyes vacant. "I guess I sort of feel that way, only it's me I feel owes something."

"Oh, really. And what's that?"

"I don't know. Being here. For her. But I'm not really, you know, not the way she wants."

"I see. And it's the blonde, is it?" Lamont motioned his chin toward Sally. "She seems to thrill more when you're squirming if I have it right. But hold this stance a little longer and she'll be over to you. Meanwhile you keep me company. I like the somber type. Besides, there will be someone here soon who will go red-faced seeing us together. My boy Vlad, you know. It takes enough to get a Russian to admit he's gay, and then to play with him like this. Things will be hot tonight."

Peter nodded and lifted his empty beer can to his mouth. "You care for another?" he asked.

"Yes. Yes. But you stay here and let me buy you one. But *do* stay."

Peter stood watching the dancers, thinking about how much he really hated the place, how he'd almost rather be locked up than be there at that moment. It was bullying him, pointing its finger at him, at how little sense of belonging he had in this world he had tried to make himself a part of. He was all flesh, heavy flesh at that, the kind that seeps down to the floor dragging its thoughts with it. The others seemed to be made of other substances—poses, ideologies of rightness and hipness he could never shape himself into. Every group had its motto, its banner flying, and his own and only was: I'm tired. He felt if others would just leave him alone he'd be able to find something else, that faint pulse barely ticking beneath the riot. But the finger pressed against his breastbone, putting pressure against his center near his lungs and heart, threatening to collapse him inwardly. It didn't matter who you were aligned with, it said, as long as you are. There was no place for the stranded, the speechless, damaged ones without affinities. You must be maneuvered. You must find home. It pressed him hard and he realized he had no place to go and that he would disappear if he let it continue. He wanted so much to grab onto something and climb out of himself, to pull and drag what was feeling the pressure out of its living carcass and to continue to rise on each branch or rung until he was gone completely, into a world of no feeling and no form. But there was nothing to hold on to, as he was held in place only by the floor and whatever it was that was trying to crush him.

He had no choice but to become hard and press back. Sparks came, and it was over in less than a minute, but it left him hurt and angry. A flood of images whorled through him in clouds of dust and smoke, of past rejections and embarrassed years, it seemed, the face of every bully who punched him or dragged him through the dirt, through a parking lot, pummeled him into a crying rot, each girl he crushed on who had laughed away or never noticed he was there, the dreams of falling, of murderous closet monsters, of teachers and his parents yelling, of choking down the terror and tears of an awkward freakishness that followed him like a fart aura his entire life. Was it he, himself, that was sick, or was the sickness merely a wall covering over the passages he tunneled through? He poked repeatedly at the sore spot inside until it enflamed. It was then that he had the first real wish he had in what seemed like forever, and that was to completely and utterly destroy the place.

He stood on the periphery of the dance floor and glared at the seemingly happy crowd and imagined their heads exploding as rays of his hate streamed out of his eyes in massive beams that struck the walls and ceiling, felling everything in massive chunks of concrete and dust, steel braces singing piercing notes as they bent and cracked. And in response, the wave of it broke back against him and he was demolished as well, all the outer crust disintegrating and out of it a minutest single flair emerged, a bodiless thing, a feeling, lightness, almost sound.

Lamont stepped up beside him and looked on bewildered in the direction Peter's eyes were cast, handing him his beer. Peter turned his eyes to the walls, blasting and felling, as the bodies of dancers went on twisting and swaying, unaware of their predicament. The images grew in strength until they flooded and overlaid, distorted those coming in through his physical eyes. All of the horrible memories and imaginings smashed into fragments that flew around him and refracted the light the music had evoked. These are *my* people now, he thought, and entered the throng with outstretched arms, a careening in a drunken ballet. And between the bodies, the spaces between them, formed yet other bodies of air, of shadow, with limbs that came and went as the throng swelled and weaved in a single substance of meat, and the energy of meat, and the energy of energy, of pure music thudding eardrums in a desperate rush. From behind he heard a voice, as if from a tiny transistor radio. "I thought you were the type that didn't like to get involved."

Peter reeled around the crowd for what may have been minutes or hours, stopping only to buy himself and Lamont beers, Lamont who had followed him around, never meeting up with his Vlad. Both of them were getting drunk, and Peter's mania was settling. He had only begun to notice that Sally had been dancing with a shirtless and muscular something or other for most of the night, and in a spasm of jealousy he approached her and grabbed her by the shoulder, planting a swampy kiss on her mouth which went unresisted because she was drunk as well. The shirtless muscle boy bobbed up and down for a few moments and then turned quickly, ending up a few feet back, folding his arms and tipping his head to talk to a friend standing beside him. Peter grabbed Lamont above his ears and kissed him on the forehead. He and Sally said goodbye to Iris and Janet, and left the club, taking their time walking back uptown.

Swaying together, wrapped in each other's arms through the acrid diesel and urine smells, they'd break apart only to tickle one another or for a mock dance now and then. It was about half way when they stopped on a corner in the thick bean musk by a Mexican restaurant for a long kiss.

Sally mumbled, looking down. She looked back up at him sadly and forced a smile.

"What's the matter?"

Sally slurred something meaningless, and tugged on his hand to get going.

Back at Peter's place, Sally hung up her coat and saw the remaining flyers Peter had been pasting up around the neighborhood. "I'm proud of you," said Sally. "I know how protective you are of your privacy. I respect that," she said with the gravity of a drunk. "I don't completely agree with it." She slumped down on a nearby chair.

Peter lit a cigarette and chose a place on the floor in the middle of a fake Persian rug. "What do you mean by agree?"

"Well, I've been thinking it would be good for you to be around people more. Being alone so much can make you a little weird."

Peter took a long drag and stared across the room. He blew the smoke out in a heavy cloud, which Sally batted away.

"It doesn't help that you keep blowing me off."

"So what am I supposed to do, come crawling into your fucking shell with you? I've got my weirdnesses. I don't always need yours."

After a long silence Peter slid himself in front of her and held her calves as he looked up toward her eyes. Sally had her face turned toward the wall, but moved her head fractionally as she looked over the table and let her gaze fall on Peter's hand, which had begun rubbing her thigh. Her arm lifted from the table and her palm landed on his wrist. Her eyes were big and sad. They raised themselves and met his and she smiled uneasily.

"You frustrate me so completely, I...," she said, thrusting her hands upward. She flung them at the sides of his head, grabbing and leaning over to kiss him on the forehead. He rose to meet her lips.

"Stop worrying. Just love me. That's what I want."

"I do. I do love you. Probably more than you'd imagine, considering," she said, hesitating for a moment. "I just don't like myself sometimes when you're around. That's all." She brushed her hair aside and looked into his eyes. Peter reflected how different she appeared now from the self-possessed image in the picture frame above his desk at work. She leaned her chin on her hand and squinted between curtains of hair. Then her face relaxed and turned to a smile.

"What?" Peter asked, leaning back to get some distance.

She said nothing, but kicked off her shoes and began scratching the instep of one foot with the heal of her other. Soon she was stroking the inside of his thigh with her toes, and then his crotch, looking at him directly, void of expression. Peter resisted. Something had to change or she was eventually going to drive him crazy. A faint, nearly imperceivable smile crept over her face, like a late afternoon shadow, a favorite of his—secret, invitational, alluding to abandonment. She was giving him what he wanted and needed, but was it really anything? He would pretend not to notice. A little longer. Frustrate her just a little bit, take some of her power away, and next time it will be easier.

Not a limb of his body moved, but the muscles in his arms and back had begun tensing. She had no power over him. She lowered herself into him, wrapped her legs around his back and nestled in. She had no power over him, he said again to himself. He felt the softness of her thighs juxtaposed with muscular fiber. Their mouths cupped, her cheeks sinking with the force of suction against his, drawing him in, the tubes of their bodies connecting, aligning in a biologic love.

The pressure and heat had begun to reproduce itself, spawning families of little flames that spread throughout his body. He always thought of himself as an awkward lover, always looking for distraction, always at the threshold of overexcitement. He had tried counting backward from one hundred, but it reminded him too much of what he did at work, and everything else he thought of eviscerated his attention. He put his arms around her back and squeezed, and she let out a breath of air, and they rejoined lips. Letting his head rest on her shoulder, he tried to think of something else, anything, and turned his attention to the first thought that struck his mind, but that was somehow in tune with what was happening in the moment. His soul was a woman, he thought, as it flashed through his mind, but what did he mean by that? He wondered harder, at the complexity of his relationship with Sally, with women in general, and they blended into an image, a composite of all the radiants of feeling that seemed to converge into a singularity. Not a symbol for all women, in an over-generalization, but an imaginary of his life as a woman as he moved through life as male, but still with an identity that merged or connected with each one of them, allowing for that to happen on a very quiet feeling level he barely understood. She stood over a cliff where he could be the first to see the sun. Around her was a circle of torches throwing flickering tongues and specters on the nearby crags and twisted limbs of bushes. She sang mournfully at the first rim of light to stain the edge of horizon, calling for it to appear, and as if listening it grew slowly upward and outward.

Sally unlocked herself and pulled his head up in front of hers. "Is there something the matter?"

"Nothing," he said. "I'm just trying to preserve the moment. I'm happy."

"What?" she asked, running her finger through his hair, looking intently into his eyes.

"I'm happy, I said. Aich aye pee pee why."

"Are you sure? You seem kind of distant. Is something the matter?"

"No," he said turning his head to the floor, "I just don't want it to be over in a flash. I'm withdrawing myself, just a little."

"Shit, Peter, I'm here now. I just can't tell if you are." She held his head and stared at him intently.

"Don't worry about it. I'm here. I'm just sort of shifting my attention, you know, the way they..." Peter glazed over and fell silent.

"The way they what? You never finish your sentences. You know what they say, an unfinished sentence is like a limp dick."

"The Kama Sutra. The way they say in the Kama Sutra."

"Yeah, I forgot, all that witch-crafty sex magic stuff. A lot of good that'll do us if you're not around."

"I find it interesting, but no, it's not about sex magic, not like use sex to get something else. The Kama Sutra is a magic to bring people together, in a deeper way."

"How about me? Am I interesting, am I something you'd like to explore, or am I a practical solution for your appetites, or just some interesting fuck for you? Solve one problem with another."

Peter went red and tried to pull himself up from under her, but she leaned all of her weight forward against him to hold him down as she pressed her mouth again against his. She tugged off her pantyhose, which peeled from her like a protective skin, and expanded in her bodiless body that filled the room, an effervescence that shifted the atmosphere.

Kneeling between her legs Peter felt his body's urgency in response to the expansiveness Sally had become, as if her matter and light, felt by some inexplicable sense rather than vision or the corporeal, had fused into a flood of an impenetrable substance, its dynamism and depth that drew all the iron in his blood to the surface, wanting only to fly from is flesh and into her shine. And just below the level of awareness, this lustful contagion had gone from mere compulsion for pleasurable spasm to a craving to know, to sink deeper into the body that was the meeting place between him and what animates and makes it move, which is her, and hear her speak in sound, a voice made for him, words just for him, the secret of Sally. To witness those gestures, expressions, and his body, his desiring body, is an obsession of molecular force, and to look on this most hidden and vulnerable part of her body, to be allowed to taste, and know her body's response to his act of tasting, to his continual tasting to experience her more, in that wordless conveyance, this was the real meaning of lust – the desire for complete transparency, while pushing past known experience. Yet this was something he could never put into words, but that he felt, and in feeling thought while he experienced it.

He lowered his head and kissed her. The hair was fibrous, and flavored lightly by salt and urine. He poured himself more deeply into Sally, into the awareness that she in her sigh and the ebb and flow of tensions, was doing the same, was releasing herself to be known, and reaching within him and receiving the knowing of him as he spoke into her.

The woman singing on the cliffside was the waking dream they made together. It wasn't necessary that Sally had the same dream, as she could have a different dream, its twin, that they were making together. And the light that shone upon her and around her was like the lust that was not love, since it asked a more singular and secret word, a word for only them, not a hollow echoing everywhere word. The woman was singing this wordless word, this time at a red, half-bent orb jutting over the rocks and sea in the distance. The flickering of the torches died down to a quiet shimmer. The sky had grown lighter. Pink, and then a royal blue above, veined in the cracks of clouds with red, like volcanic flow.

Sally sat up and lifted Peter's face, kissed him hard on the lips as they changed position. He felt the warmth of her body surround him, the enfolding of their inside-out selves staring into each other's faces. The shimmering changed to a steady cinematic surge. The song continued, not louder, but crazier and painfully joyous. The magma of the sky carved deeper, the glow broader. The sky was a full blaze of red and purple. The singing was a sweet murmur lilting off the leaves and blades of grass as the sun, in its white fury, scorched its way over the horizon. Then it stopped a moment and the woman's eyes, in the first sign of her awareness of his spying her, penetrated Peter so deeply he could feel her look flow all the way through him to Sally. Her mouth formed a silent *O* that seemed to tell him to listen deeply. To the silence. A gematria of signs composed of the particles of their disintegration. They felt their legs turn to water as a spasm shook their bodies and disintegrated, running through a flowering morass.

The two remained in their embrace, feeling the tepid pleasure of their limbs resound gently, and more gently still, slowly fading in the soft pulse of waning excitement. They exchanged a few languid kisses as they slowly relaxed their grasp of each other, pouring outward further over the bed as time passed. Peter, rolling over on his back, flicked the light switch off and smiled up at the ceiling, which was still partially lit by a rectangular column of light streaming through the window. The blankets were snowy in the blue dusk of the room. He laid back, one arm pillowing his head, one hand lying on Sally's belly. He was happy and light, and felt capable of enormous things.

He imagined himself floating upward like a miraculous bird, through the ceiling into the apartment above, and then through the next, and finally up into the sky above the city. It was still night, but the light was tweaking through at breakneck speed. The gray and black prisms below began glistening with pink edges and sparkles of white, growing louder until the eastern side of the tallest one rang each of their fierce colors, throwing hard shadows into the tranquil morning chill.

It was turning into a spring morning. The freeze was gone. The birds could be heard doing their twittering rite, and every tree imagined itself wrapped in the garlands its buds would soon become. Peter stroked Sally's stomach, and she took hold of his hand. He wished he could show her, but perhaps she was somewhere similar. He felt her sunny and warm as pink peonies against a field of green and lush willows swaying, spinning in long sheaths of silk amid the blooming mimosas. Rising up again like a feather lit by a breeze he watched the wash of light describe dilapidated rooftops and somber alleyways. It was a lonely sight, and Peter headed toward the west to see if he could spy the first bustle of Broadway. Trucks and cabs moved downtown slowly, diesel engines, and a horn now and then blanching out the bird song. A huge Ronald McDonald sat cross-legged and serene on one of the tops. Peter imagined he flew by and looked into its clownishly vacant gaze. It made him think of a time he and Sally were visiting Mona Scarlatti, a friend of Sally's from college. They were sitting in Mona's parents' kitchen, and Mona was slicing up fruit when her father came home from a hunting trip. He and his friend came in carrying boxes of evangelical tapes, and were throwing slogans about and discussing the bible loudly. Peter had met Mr. Scarlatti a few times previously, and got the impression that he wasn't well liked by the man. Peter felt he was looked at as an unwanted and demonic influence on his daughter and his daughter's friends, being young and male, with an outward rebellious pout. The two men were making a lot of noise and acting out angrily on his behalf, which was unnerving to a point, though he ultimately felt welcome, being the guest of the daughter, not the father. When the plate of sliced apples, carrots, and several types of cheeses were delivered to the table, noticing one of his favorites, Peter exclaimed with what he thought was country style humility, "Gouda! I love Gouda!"

With that Mr. Scarlatti seemed to take notice of him for the first time announcing, "Buddha is dead!"

As he drifted off, and the fantasy ran into dream, he found himself in a real estate office looking for a new apartment with Sally. He was full of delight at the thought of them moving in together. A real estate man with polished back black hair and a full double-breasted suit took them to a place a few blocks up from where Peter lived, in a small section called Funerealville. The area was lush with trees, flower boxes, brownstone buildings immaculately cut, like sanctuaries in a monastic garden. Peter was so overcome by the warmth and beauty that he was almost in tears. For Sally it was just fine, just what she wanted.

"Finally," said the real-estate man, at the end of his pitch, "the really good thing about living in Funerealville is that everyone in the community gets his own key to the cemetery." He pointed his hand in the direction of a fenced-in greenery, displaying a broad gold watchband on his naked wrist. "It is only asked that everyone help keep the graves covered with flowers."

At work the next morning Peter sat back in his chair, crossing his arms self-satisfied, but feeling a little strange.

He could tell now that Sally loved him. He should never have doubted it, but until last night she was always remote when they had sex. Something changed, and it was beyond Peter's imagining what it could have been. His guess was that he should simply accept it, and not worry, although it made him anxious.

He looked up at where he had stapled the little square of woven matches and thought a while. In a way, he realized, it was evidence that he was capable of more than he usually considered. Reaching up, he carefully pulled out the staple and held the object in his hand. Little ideogrammatic serving tray, he thought, and rested it against the frame that held Sally's photo. But the picture wasn't her. It was flat, and seemed inappropriate now that it was more obvious than ever that she was not the Sally he had inside his head, but something more like himself. She was teeth, feet, words, smells; she was vaporizing, bleeding out of her plastic holder. The ever-mutating face: try catching that with your camera. It was all very mysterious to Peter, even disturbing. He couldn't quite figure out what she was. Until now it never really mattered. He never thought about it, was always so sure that he had at least an inkling, and that's what mattered. But now that he had experienced her differently, so richly, it made him uncomfortable. Before she was simply Sally, just like the girls in high school, over a decade ago, had been this girl or that. The photograph was so much easier. It stood still and was definite. He could never get Sally to do that, not now. He realized intuitively that it was somehow his own fault. He had willed it, had wanted to own her, to see through everything. A feeling of nausea went through him. It wasn't a dream after all. She was no longer what he wanted her to be – though he still loved her. Right? She was now herself, and he was he. The recognition imposed itself on him and he paled with morbidity.

With a flick of the power switch Peter set his PC rattling and grinding. He had wasted enough time dithering. Time to get to work! Out came scraps of paper covered with notes, graphs, and coffee stains from his top desk drawer into his jittery hands. Should he marry her? Wait a minute – here it is. He pulled out a folder containing his A-1 priority project, the one he saved for such emergencies. This is it. Yeah. They'd go for it—fewer fugues and sexual dysfunction caused by a newer antidepressant medication. Peter was always on a mission of sorts, and here was another right in front of him.

"Is that the Opinions Analysis, or have you just been drawing pictures again?"

Startled, Peter twisted in his chair like a spring unwinding from the bottom up. It was Dave slouched and grinned-up in his most unthreatening of selves, a disguise which tended to make Peter tense. Mind-fucker Dave was never very clear about how playful or serious he was being. Besides, there was still the shadow of Monday, the big opportunity bartered off to drunkenness; could mean trouble-shooting and memo-writing for eternity, *loss of employment, homelessness, humiliation.*

"Yeah, this is it. It's stuff I've been working on since, uhh..."

"You mean, since then."

"Yeah. It's a little…" He waved the papers in the air and searched for the right word, "undeveloped. It's still a rough draft. I can explain it to you if you want."

"Undeveloped? Ha! It's a fucking mess, and so is this desk. I don't understand how you can work like this. But you do—I guess. Sometimes I expect you to pull a rabbit out of your hat. I don't see a hat, but there could be one under all this shit."

"Well, you see this line…"

"No. Stop. That's not what I'm here for." Dave straightened up like a general. A wisp of hair on his forehead almost seemed to be blowing in a breeze. Peter looked up at the ceiling to see that it was caused by an air duct. "I just wanted to make sure everything was all right between us. As far as the threats go—I have to make that stick—it's part of being a boss, that's all. But I still appreciate you. I want you to know that."

"I understand. Look, I know I fucked up. You don't have to apologize to me."

"Oh, I'm not."

"Hmm… It's just that my brother, he was passing through the city on his way home from Pittsburgh. He called me before he left and we planned to go out for one drink. Just one! I would never have planned to do what I did. No way. It's just that… I guess I was having trouble with my girlfriend. We talked. We drank. It got kind of disgusting."

4

Peter juggled his packages trying to fish his keys out of his pocket. He heard the last ring of the telephone just before the answering machine sprang to life, barking in a synthetic variant of his voice that he was not home, but if anybody was interested in the apartment, or anything for that matter, please leave a message. Then came a whimpering tweet and a muffled voice. Peter retrieved his keys but dropped them to the floor, accidentally sending them down a flight of steps with a swift, slipping kick. Down he lurched spastically, almost knocking over a woman and her little girl. "Excuse me!" he belched, squeezing into the corner to let them go by. The woman held her hand over her heart, breathed deeply and proceeded down the stairs in a steady march. Scooping up his keys he wheeled around and ran tap dance up the steps, hearing the click and beep of the machine before he could get the door open.

Entering the apartment, he dropped the bags of sponges, mops, toilet paper, cigarettes, vitamins, dish washing detergent, and roach killer on the dusty floor, and raised his hands behind his head to stretch. He slipped out of his coat and loosened his tie, looming over the black and gray box while he flicked on the light. When he punched the playback button the tape whizzed back and came to a popping halt, then started to play.

"Hello, Peter. This is your father. I just wanted to call and remind you to call your mother tomorrow. It's her birthday. Please try not to forget like you usually do."

The second message was from FrankFrFrFrankLin, the guy who called earlier in the week about sharing the apartment, but Peter hadn't returned his call. Something about him bothered Peter, but he couldn't put his finger on it. Was it a mild sarcasm he detected, or just the affected stutter that mimicked a digital delay? Whatever it was, Frank didn't sound like a person he especially wanted to get to know. He didn't want to be toyed with.

He sat for a while, letting Sally come to his mind. Was she too gangly? No. A lot of upper-class waspy chicks are built like that, though it was less common amongst suburban mutts. It shows she had some good blood in her somewhere, unlike himself. He tried to conjure her image, but it would come and go. One moment she was there and the next, gone, or warped by the alternating forces of anxiety and desire. It was hard to hold an image in the unruly chattering in his head, and among the nervous ticks of his body. So many times it wasn't quite Sally. It was Sally combined with his math teacher from ninth grade, or Sally and a girl he once had a crush on but never spoke to out of shyness. Sometimes these hybrids were good enough, but usually they just frustrated him.

There were so many drawings he had tried to make of her, but he wasn't much of a portrait artist. Actually, he wasn't much of an artist at all, but he had kept it up since discovering that it was a harmless, and sometimes pleasant, way to while away hours. So many of them were nothing— felt pen on yellow legal pad, or pink order-forms from work. They cluttered up odd nooks of the apartment, or got mixed in with stacks of mail or magazines. Besides the ones he made of Sally there were various animals, trees, buildings, monsters, alien beings, and then there were the diagrams of the way he thought his mind worked. He would occasionally find inspiration in the idea that if he could create a schematic, he might find out what was wrong and fix it. It wasn't even the computer programmer in him that got him going on this project, but after having spent unreasonable time alone he fell under the spell of the notion that art was a form of medicine. Out of the smatterings of occultism and psychoanalysis he had read, the Freud and Jung and Crowley and Gurdjieff and Erikson and Rogers and Skinner and Blavatsky and Horney and Lacan and Regardie and Miller and Khan and countless others, including a great deal off the paperback self-help pile, all that being your own best friend, and pulling your own strings, and winning through intimidation, he concocted his own recipe for therapeutic activity that involved, mainly, drifting further into fantasy, masturbating when anxious, and drinking to avoid desperation.

The drawings he made of Sally were more a form of reconnaissance. He had been hoping that his unconscious would yield information about her that would get him more of what he wanted. He would let the felt tipped pen drift across the page and do whatever it wanted to do, making whatever connections it made without too much interference from him intentionally. Or they were cartoon figures which he let himself draw absent-mindedly. His theory was that there was something like a magnetic field around which all the bits and strokes would accumulate into a discernible pattern that would yield insight about Sally, about himself, about his own desire and the underlying schema of their relationship.

Of course this entire exercise assumed he knew what he wanted, which was not something he was quite sure of, but since he spent so much time thinking about her, chasing, and trying to please her, it seemed that there was ample evidence that she was in fact what he wanted. But what did that mean? Nothing in him had formulated any notion of permanence, though its opposite, the idea that their being together was just a passing phase, and that he could not rely on her being there for any period of imaginable time, was not something he liked to think about. And though he pushed that bundle of thoughts out of his head, they kept lingering back on the periphery, always close enough to inspire anxious feelings anytime he was or wasn't with her. It was a little engine that kept him moving.

He changed into his most filthy and ragged clothes and tried to imagine the place spotless and all in order. It seemed nearly impossible. Everything was in perfect disarray. Nothing that belonged together was together. Books, junk mail, and magazines lay scattered across the floor in heaps with pieces of clothing, record albums, CDs, and empty food containers like it had all been washed up from a shipwreck. Over everything was a snow-like layer of dust, sometimes partially wiped free in streaks and handprints. The rug was faded by dust and spotted with dark stains. Against such odds Peter would usually abandon hope, or look for it out at a bar. This was a type of stress he wasn't used to putting himself through. He stood up swaying, feeling slightly faint, and realized that he would need more help, so he put on his coat and set off quickly to the corner grocery.

A cluster of youthful vagrants teemed outside the shop. Peter moved through as covertly as possible, not wanting to provoke a loudmouth mohawk or pseudo-lycanthropist begging for change into insult flinging, since it would eventually include everyone, and make him the center of attention. The sudden swing toward extroversion would make it impossible for anything but barhopping, and then he wouldn't get anything done at all, probably for days. The temptation to swing at a skateboard punk was almost irresistible. Peter centered himself, and focused on his goal, the purchasing of an inexpensive, but not too rude six pack, and threw himself at it.

5

Some few days later Peter found himself, sitting at the office, once again marveling at the cathode box on his desk, the face of the thinking machine he had newly acquired, since he had been chosen to pave the way into the digitized era for his department. And why not? His time was cheap enough. He would often trance-out trying to figure out what it was with these machines anyway. Were they intelligent, after all, and was the one he was staring into on his desk actually staring back at him, or was that merely his paranoiac delusion. Not *paranoid*, but paranoid-like, since it wasn't anything nearing psychosis, but an openness he attempted to believe he had about things. The machine, however, almost seemed to have an intuition, and would often get stuck on things the same way he would, though possibly for different reasons. At his most inward moments, when he was most open to possibility, and therefore to thoughts resembling *the paranoid*, though only parallel in content and structure to the actual diagnostic model, he even had the inkling of a belief, with some reservation, that the machine was jesting at him, that it had a superior sense of humor to his, possibly a superior, though obviously faster, intelligence, and this thought made him sink into a sour, shrinking state that punctuated all progress like the wall of a foundation a mole had run into on its merry way. He was just about at the point of stupefaction when his phone rang.

"What?"

"Boy, what's the matter with you?" It was Sally.

He briefly listed a number of distractions that had been forced on him earlier in the morning: Dave had sent him out for coffee because his secretary was out sick, and Marion, the receptionist, was at the doctor. When Marion came back there was a delivery for the water cooler, and since they had changed temp agencies, and all the temps were new, she thought it wasn't quite right to overwhelm them with such a task. Horace, the late sixties year-old clerk, had fallen asleep in the men's room. Three printers ran out of paper. One had jammed, and Peter had to take it apart to get at one little shred that kept it that way. The water delivery man had broken one of the jugs, which had to be dealt with right away because the water was seeping into the carpeting and into the network cabling below. A quarter of the office's terminals had gone down in the meantime, which he had to contend with while trying to dummy up three graphs Dave needed for a meeting he was late for. Last, but not least, as he was trying to bring up a terminal for a temp, she received a call from a friend, telling her that her boyfriend, it turns out, had been married all along. She ran out of the office crying, and hadn't returned, which meant he had to finish the work she had been doing before getting down to the monthly accounting, since the accountant had been out on a "Nervous Disability."

"So I guess I caught you at a bad time."

Peter sagged into his desk, leaning on his elbows. "Nah, not really. I can always get back into it. So what's up?"

"I have something to ask you."

She told him that her parents had been after her for some

time to visit. She wanted to know if he wanted to come for the weekend.

Peter, half amazed, felt his heart sink.

"Did they ask you to bring me?"

"No," she said. "But when I said you were coming they didn't protest."

"Last time I spilled a glass of red wine on their white rug."

"And you left before dinner."

"I thought they'd never want to see me again."

"Peter, they liked you. I told you that."

"It didn't seem like that. They seemed extremely polite."

There was a short silence in which Peter felt a stretching and reconfiguring of his digestive organs as he held his breath. "Okay. I'll go. You just cover for me, all right?" Sally agreed and hung up. He put down the phone and forced a smile, scratching his head. The neon images stood still on the monitor as if waiting for an answer to a question. No. It was time for another cup of coffee.

When he got home, Peter looked and saw that there were no messages on the answering machine. He'd have to hang more advertisements on Monday, or when he got home on Sunday night. He pulled out his remaining fliers from under a pile of papers and magazines he had made the night before. They were wrinkled and streaked with black from cigarette ash. Dusting them off, and straightening them out, he decided they were good enough.

He changed his clothes quickly, packed a soiled-black

knapsack, and called Sally to find out where they should meet. In front of the information booth would be fine, she said. He checked his wallet and decided he needed more money. If he walked, there'd be plenty of machines on the way. Wasting no time, he turned off all the lights, locked the door, and ran down the steps.

The train left in forty minutes, so he had to rush. As he paced up First Avenue he dodged passers-by and ran between cars at the crossings. The traffic was heavy and it moved thunderously fast at times, only to halt at one light after another. His heart began mimicking its rhythm, and he checked every storefront he passed for a clock. Ten blocks up he saw one on the wall in a cleaners. Time was running short. He began to panic and felt like he wasn't sure where his feet were, if they were with him or a couple of yards behind him.

About half way to Penn Station he realized he wouldn't have time. He started signaling to passing cabs, but none were empty. When he didn't see any for as far as he could see down the avenue he turned and fled, feeling his limbs becoming light and weak. Whatever he did, he couldn't miss the train. It was most important not to make another bad impression on the Cantors. He saw their faces floating in the air above his head, looking down at him with frowns of disappointment.

He flew across Thirty-Third Street, dancing through the traffic. Down he went over the stairs weaving in and out of the crowd and came crashing onto the floor, the snapping of his sneakers alerting everyone of his arrival. Startled commuters scattered out of his way as he lunged toward the next set of stairs, but he stopped, noticing the clock overhead that told him he had ten minutes. She can wait, he thought, and spun around back to the ATM he had just passed. There were only two people waiting.

He fidgeted and paced over a three-foot patch of dirty tile, counting each breath he took from one to ten, and over again, to keep his mind from racing. But the time seemed to stretch like a huge and bilious helium cloud inside his head making him dizzy and perplexed. Finally he got to the machine, and he tried to punch in his code, and was successful on the third try. He took out far more money than was necessary and ran out to meet Sally.

"There you are," she said. "I was getting worried. Hurry up. Here, I bought you a ticket."

He took it into his sweaty hand and pressed his dry lips into her face as they rushed toward the stairs to the platform. Running down the steps, he tripped over his own feet, but caught himself as he landed three steps down.

"Geeze, you okay? Watch yourself," said Sally catching up to him and putting her hand on his shoulder. "You'll break your head wide open on one of these stairs if you don't."

"Yeah, I'm okay." He found pleasure in this, her caring for him this way, although the idea of a gaping crevice in his skull gave him a vague chill.

The train was crowded and they stood for the first part of the ride. Beside them was a woman with a baby in a stroller who smelled like it needed a diaper change. Peter realized then that it was probably the restroom, which was only a few feet away with its door open. Both were used to riding these trains at all hours of the night, when the toilets were stuffed and the sticky rank of stale beer filled the air. They were lucky the heaters were on low, as not to agitate the air any further. He began to recognize the smell of pizza drifting in from somewhere in the middle of the car, and hotdogs with sour kraut, and burnt pretzels. All of these odors coalesced into a faint smell of rotting garbage, which was familiar enough to Peter.

Sally was looking at herself in a hand mirror, rubbing a spot on her lower lip that seemed swollen. He adored the clumsiness with which she dealt with her face. He leaned over and pecked her on the forehead, settling for that for the time being. She glanced up briefly, raising the corner of her mouth in a half-smile.

"So, what'd you do?" Peter asked.

"Oh, I was talking on the phone while I ate lunch today, and I bit myself. That's all."

"How did you manage that? Most people bite their tongues."

"I'm especially talented, that's how. That's why you love me." She dropped her mirror into her bag and rubbed his head.

When the train got to Jamaica Station people got off to switch, and before the next bunch flocked in Peter and Sally took two seats facing each other in the corner of the car. Sally went into her bag and pulled out a book and started reading. Peter rested his head back and felt the vibrations of the train in his whole body, reminiscing about the days he commuted on these trains. He thumbed the edge of his paperback and the pages flipped like a deck of cards. Over and over he repeated this, listening to the quiet zip. He fell asleep and dreamed a big man was trying to break his skull open with a jackhammer. When he woke up he found he had toppled over, and felt the vibrations of the window rattling against the side of his head.

Their car was waiting at the station when the train pulled in. It was part war tank and highway patrol vehicle, with its windshield swept back reflecting the roof of the train and the sky. As they walked toward it the image of Sally's mother smiling and waving behind the glass grew clearer through the glare. Mr. Cantor sat reposed and grinned when the door opened. Sally hugged and kissed her mother, and then stretched behind her to greet her dad. Peter smiled and put out his hand to Mrs. Cantor, and was pulled to receive a kiss on the cheek.

"Oh, it's good to see you again, Peter." She flapped her wrist after letting go of his hand, placing her fingers on his chest.

"It's nice, you having me. Thanks."

"Hi Peter." Mr. Cantor turned over his hand ever so slightly with his fingers extended. Peter reached. His hand was large and muscular, but his grip was limp. Peter looked at him intently, trying in vain to make or gain an impression. His eyes were the very rich blue of his daughter's. His hair was whitened, but full and coarse. It accentuated his reddish tanned skin. Mrs. Cantor, Helen, had her daughter's blonde hair, but her eyes were a cat-like gold on amber, like a star sapphire, though more velvety. He had trouble looking away whenever they caught his. It was always this way. She seemed to be aware of this and invited his stare with a friendly wince that terrified him.

They both climbed into the back and the door slammed behind them. As they pulled out of the parking lot Mr. Cantor began talking about the previous week's ski trip. They passed through a small village into a larger town past the lights of a shopping plaza. There was a wooded residential area, and the car went winding up and down the dark leafy hills. It had been a long time since he'd been out of the city, several months at least, and a spark of delight bored a hole through his anxiety. Night in the suburbs looked different than in the city. It had been long enough that he took notice. The lights were often smaller and further away. They twinkled behind gatherings of trees that mingled and swarmed as they sped by. Even while passing through a busy section the sky was dark and wide instead of cut off in sections by cramped rows of buildings. Lastly, they passed into another wooded section and up a hidden drive to a very well-kept Victorian at the top of the hill.

As it was late, the Cantors had already finished eating dinner. Peter and Sally were offered leftovers of roast beef, boiled potatoes, lima beans, and corn. Mr. Cantor, who insisted on being called Al, had poured a glass of scotch and opened a beer for Peter, since he hadn't been able to decide which he really wanted. He should have felt thoroughly at home, but there was something awkward lurking. It always bothered him when he found in himself the urge to embrace his host's wife, and even more so if she was his girlfriend's mother. He had been watching her as she set things on the table, her gestures, the movements of her eyes, and so forth, and now the way she looked at him across the table. She seemed to be signaling to the whole household that she had some strange and undisclosed intent aimed at Peter, and he was simmering with paranoia.

Sally had hunted through the refrigerator for whatever raw vegetables she could find and had thrown them in a bowl. She sat back and ate them with her fingers, occasionally sneaking a piece of meat from Peter, which made him feel more a part of the family.

Al was breaking up wood for kindling and tossing it into the fireplace. Helen sat at the table with Peter and Sally, competing with her daughter. Her crossed legs rode out from under her satin bathrobe, covered by nothing but a pair of blue pantyhose. Her big toe stuck out slightly through a hole, and she wiggled and circled it occasionally to make the opening bigger. Sally stood up, wiped her hands on her thighs, unlatched her jeans, and pulled them down and let them fall to the floor. A wisp of her pubic hair showed as she stretched before sitting back down again in only her briefs and sweater. She leaned over the table and resumed crunching away on a carrot. The kitchen was getting warmer from the fire in the adjacent room, but Peter decided it was best to leave his clothes on. He excused himself and got up from the table, looking for the bathroom, which he remembered was around the corner from the kitchen.

He splashed his face and dried it on a small towel, and then escaped into the mirror. It was a little dark because of the dimmer switch and his shallow pockmarks were more eerily shadowed than usual. His face was more lined on the right than on the left, and this made him look like he was perpetually turned more to one side. His hair was not quite straight, not quite wavy but took off in directions of its own without regard to decency of style. He had once tried growing a beard to even out his appearance, but it also followed no logical pattern and made him even more misshapen. For moments at a time it was an average person's face, but then it began to grow odd and unrecognizable. It happened when he looked for too long.

When he returned to the kitchen, Al was standing in the doorway, filling most of the space with his tall and heavy frame. He put his hands in his back pockets and oversaw the activity in the room. A twitch seemed to catch him in the eye as he looked at his wife.

"How was that? Everything okay?" he asked Peter.

"Sure. Fine. Fine," said Peter's disembodied voice, as he navigated the dizziness of his anxiety, pushing his empty plate aside.

"Okay. Well, when you're done I've got something to show you."

"I guess I'm done enough."

Peter stood up from the table and followed Al into the den. Beside a pile of laundry and an ironing board, in a room that was largely white and over-lit, he had a video camera on a tri-pod, a bunch of tapes and a large screened television.

"This is my new hobby. Helen gets annoyed having all this stuff around, but she rarely uses this room anyway, as you can tell. She usually watches TV in the bedroom."

"Oh. Nice." Peter bent his head downward to appear to take an interest. Al looked at him firmly, with almost a hint of anger.

"You can take your hands out of your pockets and relax," he said, raising his voice slightly. "No one around here is going to bite you." He then smiled and resumed.

Peter, who was a little beside himself, although relieved to have been torn out of gear, thought he should try to input something of his own. "Have you done anything special?" was all he could come up with.

"Mostly just friends and family stuff. I do have about a half an hour of a squirrel playing around a tree. It's kind of interesting. You want to see it?"

"Sure."

"You know, a lot of people don't like squirrels," said Al, reaching into a drawer full of cassette tapes. "Most people around here positively hate them."

"Why's that?" Peter asked.

"Oh, a lot of reasons." Al scrunched his face and thought a second. His hand went to the top of his head and hovered above, holding a lock of white-gray hair between his middle and ring finger. When it fell he began to speak again. "First of all, a lot of people complain that they eat through the electrical and telephone wires. Some say they chew apart their attics, actually eat holes through the roof so that rain gets in. Others say that they even eat away at the foundations of their houses, but I don't believe any of that crap. Maybe sometimes they'll eat through a wire or something, but they're usually not that dumb. Bats won't even do anything that stupid. And you can hear them fluttering around sometimes too. No, I think the whole thing with the squirrels started when a little girl in the neighborhood killed her little brother with her father's electric pruning shears. She'd been acting a little strange for a while. She was having angry fits in school— toppling over her desk in the middle of class, hitting the teachers, and throwing food around the cafeteria. Before that she had been fairly quiet. Not especially so. You know, just normal." He stopped a moment as he popped the tape into the slot and punched buttons on the control panel.

"Wow, so what does this have to do with squirrels? I mean, not to be..."

"Oh. I was getting to that." He stood up and faced Peter, flicking the television on as he started. "They ran some tests and found out that she was rabid, but it was too late. She died in a hospital, heavily drugged and strapped down to her bed. Poor Grizboes. What a heart-breaking thing to happen. Both kids within a month." He scratched his chin as he stared off into space.

"So did they think that she was bitten by a squirrel? Is that what this is about?" Peter twitched nervously, playing with his fingers.

Al turned his eyes to Peter. They hardened for a moment but went off into a stare again. "Yeah," he said drawing together his attention. "They found a bite mark, or so they say. You know kids. They're always getting hurt. It could have been anything. Somebody, some specialist, said it was a squirrel bite, but I don't know how they could tell. It had been festering for some time. I just don't know why nobody noticed it before it got that bad."

"Maybe they thought it was something else."

"Maybe."

Peter watched Al as he stood quietly. He seemed to be contemplating something of some moral significance. He just tapped on his chin for a while, standing tall and erect like a soldier. Peter could picture him in buckskin, tiptoeing around the forest, talking to the animals. He thought about the times he had watched the squirrels playing in the park while he was sitting at a bench, either resting or eating his lunch. He remembered being surprised when one ate through a chunk of his roast beef sandwich in a flash. He hadn't known they were carnivorous.

"So," Peter said, trying to break the silence, "what do you think it was?"

"Probably something paranormal."

"Oh. I can see why you might think that. Sure."

He watched the snow on the screen when Al turned on the VCR, flicked off the lights, and sat uncomfortably close to him on the sofa. There were a couple of flashes of white while the tape advanced. Then there was a quick flash—not more than a fraction of a second—in which he thought he saw Helen standing naked. Al seemed to sigh for a moment, but went quickly back to his long deep breathing. Peter thought it had to be her, but he knew he better not ask. Perhaps she was wearing something after all, and he had just imagined she wore nothing. Immediately following was a tree from the backyard. The camera stayed locked on it for a couple of seconds and then panned across the lawn toward the shrubs on the left, down to someone's feet, and up to the top of a tree.

With each movement it took the picture a second or two to focus, and some of the images in between were only a blur across the screen. Finally the lens found the squirrel. It focused and then zoomed in. The image bounced as if the person holding the camera was walking. Meanwhile the squirrel grew larger, and intermittently out of focus. When it was close enough so that it took up the whole picture it zoomed back again. A blurred image of a large pink hand now and then entered from the bottom holding small white objects toward the animal between its fingers. The squirrel would shy away, dance from side to side, bounce up quickly and take the food, then retreat. This happened several times until the camera jerked forward. The animal then shot to the right, disappearing into a blur of green and brown, and reappeared when the lens came into focus again on the trunk of a tree. It clung with its legs wrapped in a small arc. The picture shook and the squirrel spun and shot back down after a piece of bread that was lying on the grass, only to run back up the tree with the piece in its mouth. Then for no apparent reason it dropped the bread, ran back down to get it, and up again, only to repeat what it had just done. This happened a few times until it forgot all about the bread and started running around in circles and sometimes in figure eights, sometimes in no recognizable pattern whatsoever. Peter, who had been watching mainly out of politeness, and partially because he wanted to understand the point of it, was getting taken in. It was like watching a child at play, running around hysterically, but stranger, more exotic, and in many ways much more graceful as if it were weaving a bizarre and indecipherable script. It was like a dream. Like the grey watery phantom that spins around in his sleep. He continued to watch as the ballet grew more and more frenetic. The squirrel was leaping from hind to fore in quick, jagged motions, scampering madly from side to side, standing up with its arms outstretched, and diving on its stomach violently. The camera leveled to the ground, and lost the image for a moment. Suddenly there was nothing but a large grey blur, with a big black dot and teeth. Peter nearly leaped off the sofa but caught himself, and the grey streak disappeared into the upper left hand corner of the picture.

Al was chuckling to himself. "Isn't that something?" he said, standing up and turning on the lights. "I thought I was going to piss in my pants when that thing came at me the way it did. Playful little bastards."

"I have to admit, though," he continued after a few moments. "I peppered the bread. That's what really got him going."

That night Peter slept on a guest bed in Al's study, a fairly plain room with a desk, TV, a book shelf, and an bulbous old lamp that seemed out of place. Before he dropped off he heard something outside the room. It sounded like cloth brushing against the door. He thought about Helen, about the looks she gave him, and how she made him feel uncomfortable. Could it be her spying on him? He didn't know. It made him nervous. The sound seemed to move away and go into the ceiling above his head. There was a sound like animals scampering above him. He thought he was too anxious to get to sleep but passed out soon anyway.

As he drifted off, two large shadowy figures inhabited the room. One seemed to be male and the other female. They seemed to want something. The female shadow loomed closely carrying with it a rank sense of sexual depravity. When it got close to the bed, it washed over Peter like a wave and weighed him down. He tried to move but it held him paralyzed and his skull felt as though it was cracking. It was trying to draw something from him. Then came the male jealously to her side. They began battling, and Peter thought that he was going to die. Finally, he shook his head and almost made it to wakefulness, but then fell back down beneath them. They clashed over him and an explosion flashed inside his head.

He next found he was in a field of grass, dancing beside a squirrel who it seemed had just drank his blood and had given some of his own for Peter to drink. Something in him was dead, but he was more powerful now, and the squirrel too. It was now intelligent and could think like a human being. Peter knew that somehow there had been a trade. He could tell the way the squirrel was holding its arms outstretched toward the sky while it danced on its hind quarters. There was something strange happening, something eerie and wicked, and a feeling he was peering through cracks into something he shouldn't be allowed to see. But it somehow brought him a peace he could just barely remember tasting before. It was like being at home after school, swinging on the rope attached to the tree branch. It was a bright autumn day and the afternoon sun glistened off the last of the green leaves as if diffracted through shards of glass.

When he woke up the next day the sun came through the window and bathed the room in its liquid, pouring over his bed to the floor and the bookcase. There were several classically bound volumes glinting in gold leaf too brightly to read. Their covers were a bold reddish-brown like the clay stones he was told were Indian paint stones when he was a kid. Beside them was a worn out paperback dictionary. When he was finally done staring, he rolled out of bed and pulled it off the shelf. Running his thumb over the edge he fanned himself with the flipping pages. *Squirrel*, he thought, and absentmindedly looked up the definition.

But it didn't describe the squirrel he knew, as no dictionary ever would. These people know as much about squirrels as they know anything else.

And it made him think of the tree he used to climb to escape from everyone, his parents, even his friends. He'd climb to the highest branches that could take his weight, where anyone passing by in the woods could not see him. He'd sit there endlessly, feeling the breeze, listening to the voices of the leaves in their crisp hiss. It was his special place above the world, and he would often imagine the branches extending endlessly in all directions, with no one trunk or set of roots, just branches going on and on where he could climb to all parts of the world without another soul knowing where he'd been.

No, the people who write these books know nothing about squirrels, and not trees either.

He got up out of bed and noticed that the lamp was broken.

6

When he arrived back at his apartment, some days later, there was another message from FrankFr-FrFranklin. Was this guy kidding—was he that ostentatious, or was he simply a stutterer par excellence, whose only symptomatic tic manifested in the uttering of his own name? It annoyed Peter either way. And it annoyed him that no one else had called; what with the deal he was offering on the share he should be celebrity material. It was only typical that Sally hadn't called, even amid their newly fanned fire, but what about the rest of his prospective roommates? All, or nearly all, of his flyers had been torn down, even the newest batch—he had checked on them in his turns through the neighborhood. It was at times like these Peter began leaving himself messages, during the periods of dead air. It was a form of maintenance. He had watched his circle of friends thinning out and shredding, not sure he regretted it. Most of them had become difficult people. A lack of social life was no sweat, but it was the stillness that got to him, the coming home to a feeling no living person resided there, so easily alleviated by the blinking of the red light on the answering machine.

In place of ordinary conversation Peter had developed a hobby that he found quite satisfying, though it was a guilty pleasure since it yielded nothing. Nothing to show or talk about anyway, though he was quickly mounting piles of yellow pads, which he had stolen from work and covered with drawings and notes in felt tip pen. It satisfied a childhood urge to be *scientific*, in some intangible way. There was an illusory ambition ruined once he had gotten old enough to see how much effort he would have to expend to transform it into something practical. So the drawings allowed him to do what it was he had actually wanted, to wield his childish knowledge in secret, which was to ask himself questions, let his mind drift in a semi-disciplined way, but in a way he approved of, without a rigor which would zap the pleasure of it.

Sally thought it was a waste of time, but Peter believed his time was his to waste. Personal satisfaction depended almost entirely on waste, in fact. People accumulated wealth just to waste it gleefully. Very rarely would someone be happy doing something useful. And those who would should be called into question, possibly be locked up, since it was they who did the most to ruin everyone else's reputation. Even sex, for the most part, was a waste of bodily fluids and nutrients. In fact there was something nearly sexual about this activity of his, which made it electrifying for Peter. The ink from a fresh pen would pour out effortlessly, with the least amount of pressure against the paper.

He'd sometimes draw figures—cartoonish freaks and animals, even attempts at nudes—but most of what he drew were maps. Treasure maps, maps of ideas, maps of his day at the office, his *mind*, oozy and scattered as it was. But his most recent subject was Sally. He may have had a mind of sorts, but Sally had a *psyche*, and that was something else entirely. Not that he knew what the difference actually was, but he knew keeping that distinction worked for him, even in overtly practical ways. Their relationship was just about kaput before he turned to her as a subject. In an emergency he focused all his attention her way and saved them. He knew he was responsible. He hadn't gotten her down yet, no way, but the effort itself yielded results he could not have predicted. Sally never would have made such an effort.

And through this hobby he began to realize that FrankfrfrFranklin was growing on him, just because two or three times over the past couple of weeks he had come home to a blinking red light instead of a blank staring eye of the answering machine. There was a percolating, red planet spiraling down to him on the *starfield*, which was an accumulation of the week's drawings laid edge to edge on the floor of his apartment.

Peter's imaginary interview with Frank:

Peter: Why is it that you stutter your name the way you do?

Frank: It is because I know I am more than one personality, some being an echo of the others.

Peter: I see. So you want to give each a chance to speak. And in unison. Because you are also one, a tree with many trunks and root systems, a family of sorts.

Frank: Very perceptive. Not each actually, but a representative from each group. There are too many.

Peter: Ah, I see—a very wise thing to do, to maintain balance. A democracy of parts, with a system of representation.

Frank: Great minds think alike.

Peter: Likewise.

But when the two actually did meet, Frank wasn't at all what Peter had expected. He was much quieter. Athletic, but dorky; no threat whatsoever. Frank was at first the partially-lit figure walking down the sidewalk, as Peter leaned out over the stoop of the apartment building. He came inside and said barely a word, but listened to Peter gloze on and on about why he needed help paying the rent, the wasted space, and the unaccountable though resulting waste of time due to direct causal relationship between time and space, not to mention space-time, his own notion of what that meant. Peter told him about Sally, the great love of his life, and how this turning over a new leaf was a small sacrifice to her, or rather to them, and Frank seemed to understand, in his unspoken expression, the lamplight across one cheek in the all but dark room.And it turned out that the stutter actually *was* an affectation, just as Peter had eventually imagined, as Frank said, his "just goofing around," a habit he picked up from a *love of theater*. Peter would look back at some point, realizing he had assumed he knew what Frank had meant by *theater*, just as he had assumed many other things.

Peter was surprised, however, on arriving home from work one evening, to find a number of musical instruments, amplifiers, effects pedals, and a portable multi-track recorder waiting for him in the middle of the floor. Besides that, were a few bags of what looked like clothing, a small box of books and CD's—more what he expected.

"I know it looks like a lot, but I promise to keep it out of your way," said Frank reassuringly, as he stepped into the door behind him. "I can even keep some of it at a friend's place if you want. I have a lot of other stuff there. I just brought this from storage."

"It's okay. Keep it here. I don't mind." Peter said, hiding his shock the best he could. "You didn't tell me."

"Yeah, well, I wanted to surprise you. Here." Frank held out an acoustic guitar that he had just pulled out of a case. Peter put out his hand to say "no," as if it was a substance he was trying to recover from. Frank smiled and returned it to its case, looking over all of his belongings.

"I've got to drop off the van now. My friend needs it to take care of some things. I'll be back in a while."

Peter followed him around in a state of agitation, watching his every move. Part of him was furious. So much for peace and quiet. He paced the remaining area of floor, with his palms growing icy and damp, trying not to show his dismay. Yet there was something he liked about it, and it was this split in himself that infuriated him more than anything. Did he always have to buy into everyone else's head trip? The more he stood quietly, inactive, the more he felt the blood rising to his skull, so he volunteered to go along for the ride.

"Sure. Okay. You don't have to. Don't feel like you're obligated or anything," Frank said, pointing a sideways frown Peter's way.

"Nah. I just thought it would be nice to get out and go for a walk. You walking back?"

The van was a metallic blue, still well finished in places,

with a few dings and scratches, a slightly crumpled left front fender near the bumper. It looked as though it was about three or four years old. Inside was the sweet burnt smell of cigarettes and marijuana, and something else, perhaps burnt upholstery. There were a couple of empty coffee cups strewn about the floor on the passenger side and one crushed Burger King bag with some lettuce hanging out of the opening. Peter sat down and the seat felt comfortable and friendly to his back and backside. Frank slammed the door and started the engine. It coasted to the light at the end of the block, and when the light turned Frank shot out across the intersection and soared down the next block, veering around people and double-parked cars.

"Do you ever get yourself nervous?" Peter asked as they went hurling to a stop at the next intersection.

"A little bit, maybe," said Frank, eyes perched widely with only a flicker of a glance toward Peter. "It's discipline. It cultivates attention."

"It what?" asked Peter, not quite sure if he got that.

"Makes you stay alert."

They ended up over in the meat packing district. Peter followed Frank up to a loading dock where he opened a large metal door, and they rode a freight elevator up to the eighth floor. There the doors opened onto a small landing that had a grated metal door through which could be seen the silent flickering of a black and white TV. Ambient music played at low volume. Out popped a bearded and bespectacled head of ambiguous race, perhaps Asian, Latin, North African. It was hard to tell. "Oh. It's only you," it said, turning quickly and flinging its ponytail in the doorway.

They entered the room, which was made visible only by the sporadically shifting light of the TV. The sound was off, but its images flashed and illuminated a cloud of smoke that stretched and lingered at about chin level. An indecipherable blend of fragrances. Probably incense. Probably pot. One couldn't tell. Frank's friend lounged on a pile of cushions on the floor, and waved them in.

"This is my friend, Peter," Frank said, and plopped down. "The guy I'm moving in with."

Peter, who was already seated on the grey sofa, away from the others, stumbled to his feet and stepped over a pillow to shake his hand.

"And this is Alex," Frank said to Peter.

Alex grinned and said, "Pleased to meet you. Friend." The corners of his eyes raised with a trace of affected madness.

"You guys just stick around for a while. Okay? This is the strangest stuff I've had in a long time. I want someone else to witness it," Alex said, and held up a sandwich bag, studying it.

"Well, I really have to get back," said Peter.

"I thought you said you had nothing to do tonight," said Frank.

"I just wanted to get out for a walk." He stopped for a second, looked down at the floor, and then back up. "But I guess I'll stick around. Just a bit, then I have to go."

Alex filled a small, but beautifully carved pipe that seemed to be made of bone. When it came to Peter he looked at the images of animals, incompletely etched into its sides. Animals, demons, some childishly done, were all surrounded by primitive sunbursts and crescents, so tiny you could hardly make them out. He sucked the harsh sweetness, not pot nor tobacco, out of the mouthpiece, almost choking when it attacked the back of his throat, and studied it again. It was hard to see in the inconsistent light, but the flickering seemed to animate the images, the cartoon pantheon. Each time it made its way around, Peter would delve into it, and see more, and then watch the creatures do battle against the backdrop of his eyelids.

As it became more and more difficult to keep his eyes open, and Frank and Alex drifted further into a conversation he couldn't follow, Peter decided to start off home. He said his goodbyes, went out into the elevator and played with the buttons, but to no avail. It sat like a sleeping mouth, impossible to wake, so he went back into the next room and saw Alex dragging himself up off the cushions with a sigh and a half grin. Alex got the mouth to close by pulling a lever. Up came the bottom jaw, and down came the upper. He then yanked on a cable and the box came into motion. It dawned on Peter that it was almost as big as his bedroom, though it probably wouldn't be if the bed and bureau were there. Down they rode without a word. Peter tried breaking the short circuit in his head which kept him from thinking of anything to say; his thoughts spun tighter and quicker around a helix of what he imagined to be a dozen or so brain cells, compressing into a small hotspot in the center of his head, an itch he couldn't imagine how to get at. Alex jerked the cable again and they stopped moving. The robotic mandibles yawned with an erratic rattle and Peter dashed out a few steps, turned and waved. Alex stood expressionless. Without changing his face he tugged again at the elevator doors and disappeared.

The huge metal door slammed, and once again Peter was outside on the street. The quiet was eerie, only the buzz of the West Side Highway, and a few cars that passed down along Ninth, but no voices within hearing range. He paced slowly eastward, feeling the cobble stones through the thin soles of his canvas sneakers, his ears piqued curiously at the silence, until a bus shot by out of nowhere like a quick storm, leaving everything quieter in its wake, except for his nerves, which had received a mild and momentary combustion.

Continuing east, he listened for voices, and eventually some did begin to rise out of the desolation, murmuring nearby, he couldn't say where, a panorama of twitterings. Whose voices? The strange animals from Alex's pipe, perhaps. Once in a while a voice would sing, possibly a radio in the distance, from which he could only make out a strained voice holding a sighing note. As he reached more residential streets, the trees lining the sidewalks were like dancers posing for him as he passed, pumped full of enthusiasm and pageantry. Lights shone on them from the side of the road, from apartments above. Every concrete rectangle projected an invisible emanation upward into their branches. Stepping from one to the next he could feel how they changed in color and meaning, as if he were walking through blocks of odorless cologne.

Moving his way came a tree, very stark and not part of the parade. Its dark trunk and limbs seemed to be tightening as it got closer. A branch pointing in his direction, at his head in fact, drew the force of the rest of its body behind it. From out of its tip, like a single drop of dew, came a silent message Peter could read only through the shudder of his body. He felt invaded. For the first time he realized how intoxicated he was. It didn't come to him as a shock, though everything suddenly changed. What was that herb? There had to be some additive, something that burned at him like an electrical fire in his head. He could almost taste the smell on his tongue. Everything grew darker, and glowed with a blackness that clung like an etheric moss. The tree passing above him fell back into its inanimate slumber, and those to follow did the same. A squirrel shot down one of the trees and across his path, making him jump, then disappeared down some stairs that led to a basement apartment, as the music shifted to a cartoonish jazz.

The act of getting his keys out of his pocket and opening the locks, first to the vestibule and then to his apartment, straightened him out a bit, and he could begin to think clearly again. It was good to be back in the safety and comfort of his own place, though it was no longer so much his own. He'd have it to himself for a while, however. Frank was only getting comfortable when he left Alex's. He fell down onto Frank's bed, on a pile of clothing, and stared at the ceiling, wondering what it was going to be like, whether he'd have to kick Frank out, eventually.

He felt as though he was being watched and turned his head quickly to the window, but no one was there. He popped up onto his feet and went to see if somebody had ducked when he looked that way. Nothing unusual could be seen, anywhere in, or around the apartment, but he was being spied on. He could feel it, the eyes, though possibly not human eyes, or even animal eyes. What was it like to be stared at by stone, he wondered. Or some parasite transported into his head by that raunchy smoke. It nested in the burnt spot, a kind of sentient wave pattern which fed on neural electric currents. *That's ridiculous* he repeated to himself, as he had been doing of late, like an ad hoc mantra he mumbled whenever he found himself believing something psychotic. There was always the temptation to believe: possession, world collapsing, bending, reshaping—anything to get him out of whatever bored rut he was in.

He went into the bathroom and splashed water on his face and then looked at himself in the mirror. You're the culprit, he said to the image of his face, and shut off the faucet. You're the one's been watching me and you know it. Looking deeply into his eyes he was stopped by a morbid chill. There was a glare he didn't recognize, or that he recognized in some distant but familiar way, but had never associated with himself. A predatorial look, yet there was something else. His hair rose like smoke. It burned from behind his eyes and gave off the stink of something that had been dead for too long, yet was stalking him. It was as if something had hitched a ride in his body while he wasn't paying attention, and has since been sitting back and observing, waiting for the right moment. Something that was perhaps brought in with Frank's belongings.

He splashed his face again and buried his head in the towel, and then, careful not to look in the mirror, exited and grabbed the refrigerator door with his shaking hand and dove in after a beer. It was the only one remaining, so he checked the cupboard for something hard. There was a quarter inch of scotch in the bottom of a Dewar's bottle the office had given him on his birthday. He gulped it and cracked the seal of his beer can. It hissed a sigh of relief. Peter knew how to deal with an alien presence.

7

How did the phases of the moon affect his work? It was an unusual question to ask, granted but he had noticed in the past that it was usually the time between the half moon and the full moon that he was most irritable. Peter lay in bed feeling drugged, immeasurably more washed out than he usually did after such easy days at the office, though Dave had chewed his ear about blowing people off when they'd come asking for help. He had really blasted him, and the encounter had started a rictus on Peter's face he couldn't ignore. He had in fact missed almost everything Dave had said, fascinated by this novel facial spasm.

"Hey, a little beat, I see," said Frank. "Tough day? Lots of hard business decisions and that kind of crap?" Frank had been living with Peter for a few weeks at this point. During this time there had been intermittent patches of real conversation along a ribbon of cliché chit chat that helped to lubricate the comings and goings of the two strangers.

"Oh no. Not really, but yeah, I suppose," Peter said, more as a way of staying disengaged than communicating.

"Well, if you feel up for it why don't you come down to *The Silk Pit*. A friend of mine's playing down there tonight. Heavy stuff, a band called *Bellamonia*, I think you'd like."

"I don't know. I was kind of a bad boy at work today. I need to be fresh tomorrow so that I can undo some of the things I did."

"Fine. But still, the offer goes. By the way, I really liked your girlfriend." Frank had bumped into Peter and Sally walking home from dinner the night before. Peter had been mildly embarrassed, but Sally was undecidedly charmed though moderately horrified. "She was okay. A lot hotter than I thought she'd be, but don't take that the wrong way. I just know that a lot of hot babes are just too vacant to appreciate a guy like you."

Peter was too numb at this point to care one way or another, but a mild wave of unsettling ambivalence passed through him. "What do you mean by a guy like me?" he said, rolling over on his side to get a clearer view of Frank.

"Well, you know, you've got a lot going on inside that head of yours, interesting stuff, but you don't do PR. Most people do. They starve to have people tell them they're interesting, have original ideas. It shows in the way they dress. Too many jerks out there thinking they're the avant garde, or sex prophets or just competing to be the most cynical something or other that doesn't matter. But you get very profound over over just about anything, or even nothing. You can tell with all the shit you have lying around this place. A lot of women these days, maybe those we can call *girls*, for argument's sake, usually go for the guys who do the act. I know, because I *am* an act, though maybe not in the same way, but same rules apply. I have inadvertently made myself a target, though I try my best to avoid that kind of attention."

Peter rolled over on his back again. "I don't know what you're talking about. I don't see it. And as far as Sally goes, she's a little older than a lot of the girls you're talking about. She's a grown woman, fully, and has moved beyond those impulses you're talking about. That makes a big difference."

Frank lit a cigarette and tossed the match in the sink. "I'm sorry. I'll take care of that later."

Peter sighed. "It's okay. I'm not exactly making the cover of Good Housekeeping either."

Frank took a long drag and continued. "I don't think Sally is exactly what you think she is."

"Oh yeah? How the fuck would you know, and well, what is she then?"

"Look, I've got to be straight with you. I don't usually use terms like *babes* and *girls* first of all, but ironically that's the way a lot of women still want to see themselves, even in this day and age, and that role is like the mirror image of men, call them *boys*, who correspond to that form of mental ping pong. It's because they don't have any imagination, perhaps, and they're just acting the way they always did, the way they were taught. But you said it yourself, most of the women you know your age are in better jobs than you are, are more focused, and can probably throw a better punch than you can. That's because it matters to them, and it doesn't to you, not in the same way. Sally would likely deserve someone better than you, except for the fact that you are already better than you, and so the shoe fits."

This opened Peter's eyes a bit. "Well, shit, then who the fuck are you? I thought you were a musician, not a fucking psycho-babbleist!"

"That's not important right now. Don't worry, I'm not here to do therapy or anything, but I have to come clean. First thing I want to say is that Sally is not so fucking old and matronly. I think she's vulnerable to the same things younger girls are. Younger girls! I hate when I hear myself talk that way. Damn. Hard coming out of character at times, which I've been doing I guess since I've been getting to know you. But there are women in their forties and fifties I know who are still groupies at heart, and that suits them. It's a way of owning a little island they cultivated of their own, in this fucking big man world, and guys like me, we're just toys for some of them. And you know, I'm fine with that. My own aunt, that incorrigible beast! I say that but I have nothing but the deepest love and respect for her. She's been trying to fuck me for years now — she's a lot younger than my mother I might add. Ever since I started playing. But that's a long story and I don't want to get into that now. You just never know. I think Sally's really impressive, her way of talking, her gestures, how she moves and looks at or through people, and I believe she senses that there's something to you too, though she may not quite have her finger on it. That's all I'm saying."

"Really? Like what? That's what I'd like to know." Peter scratched the hair on his chest and began to prop himself up. "You think you know me pretty well, don't you? And Sally. You just met her last night, for chrisakes. I feel like you're playing me, but why?"

"I know how to read people, you know, specialized MI training was part of my studies at Annapolis, besides you leave those stacks of notepads around. I've taken some photos of your stuff and showed it to Alex. He's intrigued."

Peter fell backwards laughing. "I'm sorry. I don't mean to laugh at you. I'm not really. It's just that you say the most unbelievable shit sometimes." He hesitated a moment. "I didn't know you had a camera. And what are you doing in my stuff?"

"I have a spy camera. We have actually been watching you since before you put up the ads looking for a roommate. We jumped when when we saw you do it, and I drew the short straw. I had to make changes quickly, find a sublet quickly." Frank grinned, head bowed, looking at Peter out of the corner of his eye. "But about your stuff, I thought it was all free terrain. After all, you leave it lying around in your dusty piles by *my* stuff."

"I guess you're right, well..." Peter picked up the stack of yellow pads and brushed it off. "I'll get it out of your way. Put it all in some safe spot. But you, Frank, are a strange fellow, the things you do, what you say. I didn't know this about you when you moved in. It's been... interesting, to say the least. And that bit about you guys watching me, I don't even know what to say about that. I think I'm not even going to think about it. It's too weird. But you seem harmless enough."

"I know, it's all weird." Frank laughed, "but you should listen to some of the things *you* say."

"Like what?"

"No. We're alike. That's how I know. I didn't realize at first, but I have been more and more. It's a shame that you're wasting yourself. You should follow your girlfriend's example and start taking some things more seriously. I don't especially believe in things like talent, but we all have tendencies, and they are there for a reason, you know, and without appropriate cultivation they can be quite destructive. I mean this place is a mess, even after you cleaned it up, and to some degree you are too."

"My talent is maybe to create this mess you're living in, and perhaps that's both of our tendencies, so don't play that wise guy uppity role with me. You sound like you've been smoking that stuff your friend Alex pulled out the other night."

Frank laughed again, and bent over, putting his hand on his chest. "Yeah, I have, a little. I did a couple of hours ago in fact. But that's not the point, and in fact that stuff has no active ingredients at all. If you got high from it, it was just because you expected to. It was your imagination doing that to you. We smoke it because we some sometimes prefer to get fucked up on suggestion, rather than relying on external substances."

"Fuck that, the stuff got me wasted. What was it, anyway?"

"Oh, I don't know. Corn silk, maybe some sage. We call it Hey. That's H-E-Y, not the stuff horses eat."

"No, really."

"I'm sorry we did that to you. It was just a little joke. And Alex wanted to show you what you were capable of, since I had told him a bit about you, showed him your 'works.'"

"Capable?"

"It's hard to live with a creatively active person and stay dormant. Especially when you've got it in your blood. You proved that to yourself the other night when you imagined yourself into the state you were in."

"What I've got in my blood is fossilized alcohol. That's all."

"You'd maybe like to believe so." Frank grinned in a way that creeped Peter out and then shook his head, disappearing back into the other room.

Peter peeled himself up off of his bed and poked around the room with his eyes looking for something to grab hold of that might incite more than his ordinary behavior, but found nothing and dropped back down again into a comfortable delirium. He felt his limbs loosen and the shimmer go through his muscles, every click of the clock vibrating him pleasantly. Drifting off he began to see fragments of women's bodies cascade and disintegrate without coming together to form a whole. So what's it going to be? If he just laid here he would probably end up in a dreamy torpor for the rest of the night. Waste. He had wasted a lot of time come to think of it, and he looked back on many of those moments fondly as some of the happiest of his life. But life just won't leave you alone now, will it? Yes, there was still a part of him that wanted activity even though it mostly ended in disappointment. So he made an agreement with himself to give it a try once again, and got up and began putting his clothes on. It is New York City after all, Manhangover. This is what you're supposed to do. Why else put up with it?

Frank was standing in the corner when Peter walked out of the room and sat down to put new laces in his sneakers. There was an elusive expression of surprise on Frank's face, but then he smiled, and said, "I had a feeling you'd come around. But listen. Alex is going to be there. I got the feeling that he didn't go over too well with you, but that's how it is with him. He's really okay, so don't let it bother you."

Peter sat trying to decide whether to put his second shoe on.

"He's really a lot like you. He's older than I am, more your age. He was working on his PhD in clinical psych, but dropped out when he decided it was useless, said he needed to choose from a broader spectrum. He's an initiate, a shaman, in a way. But not the way you usually think. He actually learned all this stuff in the army. And since I was in the Navy, doing MI training, we ended up working together on stuff, and that's how we met."

Frank paused a moment to stub out his cigarette. "He's gone way beyond junk like Jung's archetypes, for instance. Says it's kids' stuff. He's learned a lot of indigenous trance work, deep stuff, fucking crazy stuff I can't explain, but you'll see. It's all stuff the military has been experimenting with in order to optimize training. You might think there are a lot of freakazoids in the neighborhood, believe me, you've seen nothing."

"You mean, he's a military made medicine man?" Peter rolled his eyes. "What does he do, drop a lot of acid and chant, stuff like that?"

"Well, not really, but sort of. He doesn't really do a lot of drugs, only mushrooms, peyote, you know, stuff like that. He smokes a bit. Again, it's part of his training. He says it helps him stay soft and rounded, you know smooth with fewer angles. Sometimes he does ecstasy, but that's because it was supposed to be useful at one time in certain types of therapy."

"So he hasn't thrown it away completely, all that organizational stuff."

"No. Not at all. He really believes in it in fact. It's just that he doesn't feel he needs to do a lot of statistical research and papers. We were actually working on some pretty significant projects together, especially regarding the ability to function for soldiers who experienced some sort of substantial trauma. There are these awful experiments they run at times, getting guys pumped up on various chemicals and dropping them off in places they have no business being. Or they just play the worst mind-fuck games imaginable, just to see how they react, and how long it takes for them to recover. Some don't, although some end up what they call 'enhanced,' though that's a value judgment I'll abstain from commenting on. But some recover amazingly, and you can tell because they swear up and down they'd never in a million years re-enlist – a sure sign some progress has been made.

"And then we also discovered some patients were complicated by a sort of pre-existing condition that drove them into seemingly psychotic episodes, but somehow made them more effective in certain situations that a typical soldier would have difficulty with. It was Alex who picked up on this, and it was working with one particular guy who was self-medicating with psycho-actives that drove him to his big epiphany. He was in the middle of a personal crisis himself, and he just decided to drop everything and just engage directly. He thought that instead of a distanced, analytical position, you need to get the feel of the psyche you're working with, and you can only do that by breaking habits."

"What habits?" Peter had heard this all before, but he couldn't help being curious.

"The way you experience your mind, which of course includes the sensations of your body, based on both real and imagined external events." Frank seemed to believe in what he was saying.

"So that's why he goes out of his way to sharpen his mind with that wacky weed he had us smoke. I get it. I get it!"

"No, really Peter. I think he knows what he's doing. Besides, you're one to talk. You pour down those beers sometimes like there's no tomorrow."

"Yeah, but I'm not trying to get in touch with the inner workings of my mind. I'm only trying to take the edge off of it. I never said I was any scientist."

"Yeah, but think about it. Alex says that what happens when we are younger is that we are forced to take a big look at some of our experiences, kind of like taking a photograph of it, sort of with the entirety of our momentary experience, and later those are the things we remember. For the rest of our lives we're trapped by them. They become walls that box us in, almost literally, physically, I mean. The reason you want to take the edge off it is because you don't like the way the pictures turned out. They have edges, and those edges are a bodily sensation too."

"I don't know if I understand the analogy. I was never too much into photography. But it sounds like he just wants to make everything into one big blur."

"Sort of."

What the fuck. Peter finished putting his shoes on. They can't be too dangerous. They're not stupid, that's for sure. Frank's friends were probably no more crazy than he was.

It's just that he saw slipping as something to struggle against, and Frank's friend saw it as a reason to rejoice.

As they turned down Bowery, Frank and Peter approached the crowd that was always hovering outside the welfare hotel. A man frowned at Peter and spat on the sidewalk as he walked by. Peter felt his body stiffen in the usual way, walking foolishly by like a dog with his tail between his knees. After several years of living in the neighborhood he never got used to being hated. He didn't like being blamed for everything—rent prices, homelessness, joblessness, ugliness, slavery, racism, violence, degradation, sickness, horror, the deteriorating quality of hamburgers at the Ukrainian cafe, but because of his straight white male status he felt he had to accept it. He had always managed to take shit he didn't feel he deserved, for things he had no control over, and he probably always would, no matter where he lived.

"Hey, what's the matter, Pete. You don't mind me calling you Pete, do you?"

"Nah. Nothing's the matter. Why?"

"Oh, you're just looking a little glum. That's all."

"I don't like the photos."

"Ha! I know what you mean."

It was two bucks at the door, and an X on the back of the hand. Inside it was familiar enough, stark and dimly lit, but with a nice rustic bar. They had moved the stage back again since the last time he was there. Early eighties techno-pop churned out of the PA, too trebly for ears that had just come in from outside. They made their way towards the stage and found Alex sitting by one of the few tables in the place. It was in a cozy little corner sheltered by the sound board.

Peter went to the bar to buy the first round, trying to start off creating a little good will. It took time to get the bartender to notice him, and by the time he got back to the table a woman with bleached cropped hair and pale skin was sitting in his seat. So he handed out the beers to the three of them and went back to the bar to get another for himself.

When he got back and squeezed into a seat by the corner he was introduced to Ivory, who was one of the singers for the band they had come to see. On closer look her skin had a grayish tinge one might expect of a committed junky, although she seemed quite lucid, enough so that it had an effect on Peter, who was hyper aware that he was hiding from her eyes, which were alive and probing. Peter recognized the type—with immediate dread—not that he could say what it was, but it was something that he'd felt before, if only once or twice.

"So Frank tells me you're a romantic," she said, wincing a half smile and blowing out a funnel of smoke.

"Hah. That's funny that he'd say that about me," Peter said a little nervously, taking a sidelong look at him. "I would think that would be more true of him," he continued, feeling self-conscious about the stiffness of his speech.

She looked away and took another drag, and blew it out. Looking back at Peter, dead serious, she said, "Frank can't afford to be a romantic. He has too much invested."

"I would think that he couldn't afford not to be. How else can he believe enough in what he's doing?" This time Peter felt he was getting his footing. That's right, throw it back at her. Be as clever as she is.

Frank sat back, mouth half open, half smiling. His eyes turned from Peter back to Ivory.

"If he was a romantic, he'd find all the reasons not to be," Ivory shot back, almost too quickly for Peter to catch. "Whenever he found an obstacle in his way he'd start complaining about how sad and unfair the world is. He'd start thinking about suicide. He'd be mean to other people because he felt like shit all the time. Eventually he'd end up in a union job, or perhaps one like yours."

Everyone at the table laughed, everyone but Peter that is, who was growing flustered, and maybe slightly angry. "Look," he said, slouching deeper into the table, "not everybody's as talented as you are. And not everybody has such a burning desire to prove themselves. There isn't anything I can think of that I want that much, and I would be fooling myself if I did. We're only capable of certain things. I do what I do well, and I'm happy about that. Not real happy, but happy enough."

"See what I mean?" said Frank, leaning over the table to Ivory.

"Uh huh. Bellamonia. The beautiful disease. It's what I named my band. It's a gift, in a way." She stubbed out her cigarette saying, "Look. I've got to go back now. Thanks for the beer," holding the bottle above her head as she twirled toward the stage.

"What was she giving me shit for?"

Frank giggled. "I don't know why she gets like that. She only does with certain people. I think she might like you."

"I'm sure she does." Peter sat back and folded his arms across his chest. "And where do you come off telling people things like that. As I said earlier, you don't even know me."

"Not true buddy boy. And you're the romantic, or the bellamoniac, not me."

"I don't understand. You're going to have to explain this one to me."

That's when Alex joined in. "I think what he means is that you've got a deviantly romanticized view of things," he said breaking into a smile, "the sort that's indigenous to the white American male, particularly of the suburbs, who has left the burbs looking for something, but something that has successfully hidden behind his own stupidity, and I must add, a stupidity that he himself has very carefully and intelligently constructed. It's an irony. You're a work of art, my friend." He leaned over the table and drove his eyes at Peter. "And I need to add that you have a rare and acute form of it because it conveniently includes a traditional work ethic and rote expectations, with all the trappings, but something dangerously more. And that *more* is what distinguishes you, but also grossly distorts your apprehension of your situation. And it all provides ways to avoid thinking about having to do what you don't want to do. It will only work for you for a while. Sooner or later you're going to have to find something to replace it, or construct something more foolish, though perhaps more useful. That's probably the most positive thing about it, uh, what you have right now. People like you often end up going back to religion later in life. We all need something. Such a sweet, pretty narrative. The splitting away, through life, of two main threads: of what is, and what *should be.*"

"Oh, thank you, doc. I feel like I've been summed up on a balance sheet, for fuck sakes. I almost forgot that you were the professor. Thank you. Now I know that I'll have to change. Shit. And possibly even fall back on religion because I can't stand up on my own feet."

Peter leaned back and turned his face away from the others, rocking his chair on the back legs. "Look, I'm not having very much fun tonight. I hate to be a party-pooper, but I think I'm going to get going."

Frank reached across the table and grabbed his arm. "Ah... he doesn't mean anything nasty by what he says, Pete. You can turn around and say something equally unflattering to him. He's just playing with you, even if there is some truth to what he's saying."

"Yeah, Peter," Alex broke in, "I apologize for plucking at your feathers. But it's true, I'm no better off than you are, and I'm not categorically a white guy, but more of a bundle of less typical attributes, so in a way there is an advantage to my disadvantage, a distance perhaps. I spend so much time studying this kind of crap that I feel the need to joke about it sometimes. You are deviant, yes, but in many ways the way we all are here, and we make up lies and pretend roles and practices to run from it, even though there's no escaping. You just keep running, but not the kind of running you do when you completely avoid thinking something and doing something about it. We run because it's our way of life. So the lies I tell you are the lies I tell myself, and the clowning I do as part of that lying is part of that work too."

"Well, at my expense. You don't know me. It would be different if we knew each other better."

"I'm sorry. I'm sorry. I just assumed we should include you, not leave you out, by initiating you into the way we manage ourselves and each other. And note that I say *initiation*, because that is part of the lie, but it's also something true in a way, since all initiations are a falsity, but they permeate our behavior and perceptions all the same. And by the way, maybe we do know each other better than we think. Another thing about *Bellamonia*, is it's different for everybody. Most people have the pseudo variety, and if you go back to your old neighborhood, you'd probably see a lot of regressive behavior, or just a lot of people seemingly stuck. That's how they deal with it. In your case, you have the sort that attracts chaotic influences," Alex laughed, "like us, for instance. There's a reason for that, and there's also a considerable consequence, at times, and that's what we have to guard against. You need proper shepherding, in other words."

Alex sat back and took a sip of his beer. Peter sat sullen, watching a dampened spot on the table slowly grow, he thought, into the shape of Australia, feeling one part of himself trying to drill through to the other side of the world.

"And don't worry, there's no DSM entry for it. The accepted science wouldn't have anything to do with it, as they rely on reductive statistical data, and something like bellamonia would disappear from view at the thirty-thousand feet or so they need to look at things from, which also confounds them, since they often over-generalize and provoke things like schizophrenia in patients where it didn't previously exist.

For instance, in bellamonia, there are often fugues similar to psychotic breakdown that are in no way psychotic in the usual sense. You see it in folk medicine all over the world, the period of personality breakdown before one becomes a doctor, I mean in the folk medicine sense, shamanism and so forth. In fact, the official medical profession would call what we're talking about folk medicine as well, or snake oil, even, and perhaps it is, but it seems to work for us. We are practiced observers and just name things we see the way we see them. We also don't try to cure things like this, because we recognize them as natural patterns, progressions, things one lives through and grows through. Hence, this is why we say *shepherding*. You don't require fixing, but we provide some extra rubber for your walls while you need it."

"Oh fuck off." Peter, who had been leaning on the table holding his head in his hands, sat up straight in his chair. "You're so full of shit your breath stinks of it. You're a fucking creepy dude, if I have say so, Alex. You make all this shit up about me, offering me this total mind fuck explanation of everything from the way I jerk myself off to the way I brush my teeth, and somehow I'm still sitting here. As bad as this all sounds, part of me is entertained by all this shit. Go ahead, go on with your game show. I guess this is why I'm living in this junky neighborhood to begin with, to be amused by you fuckers. You're all nuts."

Alex's eyes glared, but then he smiled and leaned further toward Peter, his voice deeper and softer, and somehow increased in volume. "Well, let me put it this way. What I was saying about you before has at least a partial truth. Do you agree? And yes, of course it's a game, but not a show, it's always a game. You don't think official psychiatry is a game? The damage they do is due to their misunderstanding of that very fact. But the consequence I mean is that you're going to at times feel as though you've gone absolutely bonkers, but that's not it at all. You might begin distorting the things you see differently, but it will all be just a different version of a delirium everyone is already sharing, or at least sharing enough common language that it's not so obvious. It's really just a human attribute, this ability to delude and distract ourselves, to interpret the world according to a certain biological and cultural slant. You're changing that slant."

"Fuck you! No! Yes! Okay. Maybe a little bit, but what's the point? I know what I am and I get away with it."

"To some degree I can understand that belief, and only because it's very much like my own default set of beliefs, I'm sorry to say. But *getting away with it* puts you in a position of having an aberration, something unacceptable that you have to hide, and what we're saying is that what you're experiencing, at least to some degree, is ubiquitous, but there is a special flavor to your experience that sets you apart, partially because of the weirdness of your behavior, but also what they say about your underlying beliefs."

"Okay… So? You think so, huh, and how do you think you know what I believe? I'm not even sure half the time I know what I believe, and I'm pretty sure there's no system to it. I believe that I have a job and a girlfriend named Sally, and I live with your asshole friend."

"Hey!"

"Sorry, Frank, I know you don't really deserve that. But it's just that your agitator friend over here is throwing a lot of bullshit at me like he knows anything about me or the world we're living in. I don't believe there are any secrets, no mysteries of the human soul anyone can impart on anyone else that will make a fucks difference in any way. There's just no meaning to any of it. We're just here, making it all up."

"So that's what you believe," Alex continued. "Yeah, we're just making it all up, but you have a beer on the table here, and you believe there is a table, otherwise you wouldn't rest your beer on it because you'd be afraid it would fall to the floor and smash, and you wouldn't have a beer anymore. And you believe that the beer has some value, and you believe to some degree that being here among other people has some value. And you therefore believe in a kind of idea of *value*, even if you don't verbalize it that way to yourself."

"Okay, but what's your point? I have beliefs that get me through my day, sort of compiled from the habits of experience. And values. Great. But you just want me to adopt your fantasies, and I say fuck that."

"Not just my fantasies, no, but what about other belief systems? We disregard things just because they don't jive with our outlook, with what we assume to be true, what science allows, what our experience, as you say, seems to suggest. So, say we decide we don't believe in a spiritual life, a soul, or say reincarnation, for instance."

"I'll go along with that." Peter shifted in his chair and cocked his head.

"Even imagine that, not only could we not prove that

those things exist, but say for argument's sake that we could prove scientifically that those things didn't exist. Would that mean that they weren't at all useful to us?"

"Well, it would be foolish to believe in them then. Unless of course you were at your wits end, and needed something to get by, to prop you up in a way. But I still don't see the point you're making."

"But what you're completely overlooking is the possibility that those things are brain functions, notions that evolved in parallel to the actual physical brain, without which other real things aren't possible."

"Like what?"

"A different sense of experience. Possibly an inner code, part of the language of the brain, or the operating system, like the DOS on your new PC, or the underlying system on a mainframe. But of course, these patterns are always in flux, shifting and mutating over time, but around a fairly consistent loci based on the physical structures."

"Huh?"

"Frank tells me you work with computers. Now imagine if you didn't understand all of the functions possible to you. Your work would be a little limited, wouldn't it?"

"Well, I'm really only a hack. It is pretty limited."

"Okay. Then you understand."

"But what does that have to do with us knowing each other?"

"Maybe it would be useful for us to pretend we did. You remember that concoction you smoked at my place the night we met? Frank told me you didn't believe that it was fake, no active ingredients at all, but yet you thought you were totally stoned, could hardly manage yourself. That's the kind of thing I'm talking about, what you're capable of."

"I still don't believe you both about that weed. No, I know when I've smoked potent stuff. I no longer do consistently, but back in high school…"

"Okay, that's not the point right now. You don't believe a word we've told you, and you don't see yourself in any way a part of what we're doing, what we're talking about. Bellamonia is just bullshit and I'm a con and a jerk-off with flagrantly stupid and dangerous ideas. But I've seen the pictures Frank took. That's a huge giveaway. Believe me, there's something going on. I implore you to listen. There are things you don't understand about yourself, that you couldn't possibly have knowledge about, and it might be helpful to pretend you accept some of the traditional fantasies, even my quirky fantasies, because they may be able to protect you from what is happening now."

One by one, the members of *Bellamonia* came out onto the stage, plugged their instruments in, banged on their drums, flicked on their amps. As they began, everyone except for Ivory played back in the shadows, while she stood alone in the spotlight. The drone of instrument noise rose as she began to chant.

I'm what you want to feel
But I am not real
You think you figured out

Your thought is hanging out
You're just baby to me
I'm just a vapor to you
You always crave for maybe
Way more than what is true
You think I am a body
But I can't be your hobby
I'm what you want to feel
But I am not real
You think you're ready for me
But I am not real
You think you're in my story
That you are the deal
You want a fantasy
And you don't want to see me

Then she looked directly at Peter and sang,

But I could damage you, damage you
I could damage you, damage you

Peter wouldn't have wanted to admit it, but it was electrifying. The room was pitching slightly, which he attributed to the quality of the stage lights. The rest of the place was quite dark except, it seemed, the little corner in which he was sitting. One naked light bulb hung a few feet above his head. There were others scattered around the ceiling, but from where he was sitting this one seemed particularly bright, especially with Ivory up on stage tossing glaring looks his way as her body began twisting and convulsing as the volume started to rise. She was a little girl, Peter was trying to tell himself, nothing to be intimidated by, but she seemed a lot larger up there, and much more powerful. The muscles in her arms and legs were tight and rippling like they were carved out of oak, and her face went through various contortions, sometimes composing itself in angelic calm, but then to malice and tooth baring snarls. He felt like he was being made love to by something rabid and out of control. Worse than all this was that he couldn't decide what he feared most. There was a part of him that wanted her, enough that he was beginning to panic. He felt a strong urge to crawl up on stage and get crushed by the intensity of the light reflecting off her face.

Then the guitars began surging, becoming ear rending as they moved into the next song. The bass was so heavy he felt it pounding on his heart, making him feel weak and dizzy. He tore pieces from his beer-damp napkin and stuck them in his ears, and ducked low over the tabletop. The lights were changing, swirling in different colors drenching in an oil slick of crackling migraine. The sound began forming a pattern, a still blaring electric guitar held a distorted rhythm as the other layered a repeated melody above it. Ivory began singing in a sweet, thin, high register as the bass player barked and growled, trying to pop the speakers. Peter felt the radiations of static electricity scouring through him, pushing everything aside like commuters pouring into the subway doors as rush hour reaches its peak.

He sat tightly, trying to hold himself together, and finally regained enough composure to sit back against his chair, until a small explosion behind his left shoulder made him jump and break one of the legs of his chair. He went tumbling back, trying to hold onto the table to steady himself. But he slipped beneath it, and it came crashing down onto his chest as he smacked the back of his head against the floor. A beer bottle struck him on the forehead, then the ashtray fell into his mouth.

The band stopped playing in about two beats, but it was a break in the song. The noises of the instruments re-converged, seemingly at him as a central point.

For perhaps the second or third time in his life he was seeing stars and found them very interesting. He turned his head towards the stage and saw Ivory standing in the shadows.

Frank asked something he couldn't hear and he paused before helping him up.

"I'm all right. I think I'm okay," Peter said.

Frank shouted, "Come on, let's get you out of here."

Peter stood up, spitting out the ashes and cigarette butts. His legs felt a bit wobbly, but nothing hurt too much, although he felt a couple of sore spots around his head. The song ended, and a hum filled the room, loud but not as loud as the music.

"Hey, why don't you sit down here for a while. Have a beer, until you're ready to go," said a bouncer meeting them on their way out and pulling up a chair next to the bar.

"No, I think I best be getting home."

Peter sat down on a stoop a few doors down. Frank walked up and stood a few steps away. They remained in that position some minutes and then Frank sat down next to Peter, asked him if he needed or wanted anything. Peter shook his head with a shudder going through his body.

"It shouldn't be too long. It's only a 20 minute set tonight, and Ivory was going to meet me afterwards. If you want, I can take you home and come back," Frank said.

"No, that's fine. I'm good. I mean, I'll be good, I imagine, after a bit."

When Ivory arrived, she turned a questioningly look towards Peter.

"You better watch it. I've seen people really mess themselves up like that." She continued to walk with them. "Sorry if you hurt yourself, but I'll take it as a compliment. Besides, I like men a little off balance. Let's go get some tea."

Peter, Ivory and Frank all sat down in a Brazilian cafe on Seventh Street. Peter ordered a steamed milk with orzata, thinking it would help him sleep. Ivory sipped an herb tea and began wiping the thin layer of makeup from her face with some cream she had taken out of her bag. Peter watched as the life returned to her face. Beneath the makeup Ivory was somewhere between marginally attractive and plain, a look that Peter found comfort in, not at all disappointing.

"So that wasn't really you," he said.

"What do you mean?" she asked.

"Your skin color."

"Oh that. It's a stage prop. But it's me. It's my design."

She put the clump of tissues in the ashtray and put away the jar of cold cream. "I guess it depends on how you look at it."

Her eyes were looking directly into Peter's as if they were waiting for some kind of signal. After a while he responded.

"Interesting act you've got. I liked it."

"I know how you felt when you were sitting there tonight. I think you're coming back."

"What?"

She crushed the tissues into one corner of the ashtray and lit a cigarette.

"You know, you are like our perfect audience. We write our songs for people like you."

Peter was baffled. He didn't know what to say, so he sat silently.

"But it wouldn't pay to play for one person, or a couple of people, now would it?"

"I guess not," said Peter.

"But that's the way it always is. Everyone else is there just for the scene. They don't understand."

"Pete, I think there's hope for you," said Frank, putting his hand on Peter's back.

"I think there is too. Don't give up, whatever you do."

Peter shook his head and laughed. "What's up with you guys? I mean, really."

8

For as long as he'd been working at the job, Peter had watched Horace dwindle from a quiet and proficient accounting clerk to a slowed and troubled presence. He seemed to be physically sinking, as if the string that was holding him upright at the top of his head had dropped inches so that his shoulders had begun to wrap and close in around his ears when he sat. And more and more, he would appear at the edge of Peter's cubicle with wide glazed-over eyes, focused at some nowhere point through the cubicle wall. Peter wasn't sure what it was. Horace didn't seem to understand his own situation to any great degree, and appeared to have momentary bouts of frustration with his inability to grapple with things as he used to. Things were getting more muddled, undefined, harder to hold on to and remember. At least that's how it seemed. Peter, who liked to think of himself as a somewhat sympathetic sort, would help Horace make his way through certain rough spots – explain the numbers, help him organize information into neat columns and rows, redo endless reports and spread-sheets for him. It had gotten to the point where Peter was doing possibly seventy percent of Horace's job.

Horace would have been retired if his newfangled pension plan had been better explained when it was changed from the old standard. There was a year or so over which these facts had revealed themselves, when he had been making his plans, looking forward to spending more time with his wife, and it had become apparent that he hadn't the resources he needed to stop working for a living. Horace needed more time, and Peter was one of the people invested in trying to help him get it. There were others, but it was Peter who was most fully committed, as he was one of the youngest in the department to remember Horace's better days. Dave pretended to be unaware of this situation, though with a wink. So it was understood on some level that part of Peter's job – unofficially speaking – was to ease Horace's last few months or years as an employee of the organization.

But Peter and Horace had a recent falling out, which in itself was something hard to fathom, since it seemed there was nothing about Horace that could possibly provoke conflict. There were a number of tasks Peter had taken on that were no longer looked at as favors – just more work for Peter. Even Horace began to think so, and it was what Peter looked at as presumptuousness on Horace's part that would enrage him to no end. There was a fuzzy line, for sure, since there was never anything definite decided by anyone, and all the changes that were being made were changes in habit and routine, rather than specified job description. But it was on these fuzzy little areas that Peter struggled most when it seemed to him that Horace no longer even appreciated that he was being helped at all.

Though Peter read him the riot act the previous day, had listed off a number of things he'd no longer do or help him with, and had actually flown into a bit of a rampage, Horace arrived at work that day seeming peppier and more upbeat than he'd been for as long as Peter could remember. This shocked and perplexed Peter, since in his mind Horace was unofficially doomed. Peter had also been a bit worried because the frenzy he had whipped himself into drove him off to a liquid lunch after that, lasting into evening. Luckily, it seemed, no one had noticed his going missing, and so that concern was soon eclipsed by the possibility that Horace might be going fully mental on him.

After some consideration, Peter decided to offer up his help again, but to no avail. Horace would have nothing to do with his help from now on. That's the way it was going to be. Peter thought, *fine with me*, but it made him anxious for the man, who had actually strolled by humming on his way out to lunch. Could it be that he suddenly decided he could help himself? After all they'd been through?

Horace was on Dave's mind when he called Peter into his office. Having noticed earlier something peculiar in the way Horace was pacing and orbiting the floor, he had asked him inside to chat for a moment. From Horace's rambling Dave surmised that he was speaking to someone deeply confused and who needed help immediately, before he popped his cork.

So when he brought him in a second time, he told Peter, he used his best managerial reality spell to get him to speak clearly, with which he succeeded to a lesser degree than he would have liked. Since the actual truth was far too complicated for Peter to explain, even to himself, he simply told Dave that he had offered his help, but because he had been somewhat critical of the way Horace was handling the job, there had been a bit of a confrontation, after which Horace refused to talk about it with Peter any further.

"Well, that's nice of you. Always the suave handler, aren't you?" Dave looked at him hotly, with the trace of a smirk. "I don't know who else I'm going to get to work with him, although I don't really understand why I have to. He's done stuff like this before without a problem. Maybe he just needs his confidence restored after what you did to him. When did you say this *confrontation* took place?"

"Yesterday. In the morning."

"Oh. Then that's gotta be it. It makes perfect sense now. Peter, don't go doing stuff like that to my employees, will you? Especially somebody like Horace. You know he's... vulnerable. Who the hell are you to come off as judge and executioner?"

"I'll tell you what. I'll talk to him again. This time I'll try to be nicer. I'll take back what I said. Better yet, I'll explain to him that I didn't understand what he was up to. I couldn't tell if he was getting inventory confused with taxes or cash flows from distribution, or something supernatural, which, all joking aside..."

"Do what you have to. I don't expect you to finish the job for him. Just see if you can motivate him a bit, and get him back to planet earth."

Peter went back to his desk. He stared into his monitor with a nameless fear that enlivened him, and tried to look busy while dreaming of how to deal with his new situation. Okay, if Horace lets him help, he thought, everything will be fine. Maybe. He'd get an extended deadline on his own work, so that won't be a problem. There might even be a little extra free time.

On the other hand, thought Peter, if Horace refused his help, he could get his own work done, and could get home earlier and nap away the last of his hangover before Frank got home. But Horace would more than likely only spin his wheels into further spirals of the surreal, make no headway, and Peter would get blamed for it. He took down the little square of matches from his wall and ran his forefinger over the weave while he waited for an idea. I just have to go back and talk to him, maybe take him out to lunch, make up to him somehow.

Peter made a few more attempts, but each time he approached Horace's cubicle he was either not there or had grown completely silent and unwilling to communicate. When Peter walked away after his final effort that day, he could hear that same eerie humming start again as he left the area. But he was resolute and decided he still had time to fix things if he let some water under the bridge and start out again first thing in the morning.

The next day, however, things took a turn for the worse. The amount of paper on Horace's desk seemed to triple in just a few hours. By the afternoon he had gone through half a dozen legal pads, all of the pages covered with uncanny diagrams and notes that seemed to have nothing to do with his work. But when he looked closer Peter could see parallels with his own approach. Among them was a diagram of the earth and two moons. The second moon, according to

Horace's notes, was ordinarily visible, though was a only a complete replica of the first. The problem was that, because people were two eyed beasts, they made them both into one and disregarded the original out of moral ignorance. The lost accounting figure that Horace was looking for was on the original. Another diagram was a plan for a supposed telescope that Horace would build in order to find it. Oddly enough he had found it. Peter had checked it out. It was written alone on a piece of paper with rays emitting out of it, and a blurb beneath it saying, "The Lost Number." Somehow Horace had tackled a major obstacle, but seemed to be more interested in the nonsense he created around it than in completing the project altogether.

Later in the day, Horace appeared happy and friendly, more so than he had been over the past few days in fact. He said little, but smiled a lot when he wasn't rifling spastically through the papers. It all made Peter a little nervous, the way he seemed to be heading downstream without a rudder, and seemingly making progress all the while.

A few days later Peter arrived at work and was told that Horace had died of a heart attack. His first reaction was a cold tremor that went all the way through him and froze him off to the rest of the world. He sat down in his chair, stupefied. Receding to a point, alone and silent, he wanted desperately to sleep. He sunk more deeply into his chair and gazed blankly across the room. The cloth pattern in his cubicle wall shimmered almost unnoticeably, and after some minutes began to form a variety of geometric patterns, then insects, protozoa, maps of ghost cities, pixilated versions of the drawings and diagrams he had made to generate ideas when he was stuck. What would it be like, he thought, to inhabit any of their landscapes, those flat worlds constructed of interconnected dots? Would it feel different, having lost the third dimension, space itself, and everything that occupied it? What things was a body prone to that an abstraction, a conscious abstract, would not be? Perhaps there was an extra-dimensionality to those worlds, a space folded in and around space, beyond human perception and reckoning, and possibly a whole new set of discomforts, perhaps sharper and more persistent than those inconsistent and amorphous clouds that shifted through his own presence. The barely perceivable images might be the only portal now between this world and where Horace was, the flat and cartoonish interface between them. And if Horace was in fact occupying that world, was he preferring it to this one? Were there things that existed there that could make it worse for him, or was it an escape from the pain that could only exist in the flesh? And if there were unfortunate things, entities say, even monsters, could they pass from that world into this? Now that Peter had formed a connection, could they interfere and cause disruption in his life?

This *was* disruption. This passing of part of his known existence into the non-existent. It happens when the portal opens and something gets scooped up and sucked in. Peter sat, it seemed for days, dissolving into a mist of infinitesimal specks through which various forms of magnetic and electrical waves ran, and something else, something native to that other world, as he began to bond to the interface, the geometric spiders and worlds through which he would pass.

9

Peter glozed through the next week in a numbed and withdrawn state. He had seen Sally a couple of times, but it had been difficult being around her while in his state of mind, not feeling inclined to give or receive affection, nor to talk much. Frank was thankfully away from the apartment most evenings, rehearsing, recording, hustling for gigs, or out with his friends. At home, there was plenty of isolation time for trying to read, staring at walls, and occasionally drawing with his felt pen on legal pad drawings of pixelated spiders, ghostly forms, monsters. A couple of nights he may have drunk too many beers by himself, which distracted him through difficult recovery-mornings.

A few days after Horace died, and the office had settled into its post-shock state of *morbidity lite*, Dave stopped and lingered by Peter's desk, watching him for some moments. "Do you have a minute, Peter?" His face was sober and relaxed, but with tones of gray. He motioned his head for Peter to follow.

Peter pulled himself up out of his daze and followed Dave into his office, feeling a light anxiety penetrate the giddy hollowness.

"I just wanted to talk about what's been going on here," Dave began. "I was afraid you might be feeling a bit guilty, and I wanted to assure you that you're not responsible."

"I don't think I am." Peter paled as a tremor when through his back.

"Okay, that's good. We had that talk the other day. I know you might have reasons for blaming yourself. I'm probably the only person who knows about your relationship with Horace, how you basically pulled him through over the past couple years. I never said anything because it was working. I can say it now. You held him together as long as you could. I just wish it never had to happen, but I didn't see any other way around it. So, if you feel a bit like you contributed to this event, I just wanted to assure you that you are not alone. I feel on some level it was intentional on both of our parts."

"You mean . . . you? We?"

"Yes."

Yet there was probably nothing he could have done about it, Peter realized. Something like a pile of ash came to rest on his shoulders, and a sharp poke landed in the middle of his chest. The more he tried to wrestle it into submission, the more resilient he found it. Part of him was angry about it all, angry that Horace had gone ahead and died just like that, not caring about the unalterable circumstances he'd create along the way. And in his anger he was glad that he was dead. The little shit deserved it if he could just go out like that, without any warning, without giving any signs so that everyone could get out of his way. Peter tried curbing his malice by thinking of Horace's wife, poor, sweet, old Mrs. Stochastiki.

"You knew all the time that I was covering for him?"

"Yeah. I guess you could say that I was covering for him too."

"But why? And why didn't you ever say anything?"

"Well, if I admitted it I wouldn't have been able to let it go on now, would I?" Dave smiled. Possibly the warmest smile Peter had ever gotten from him.

"I just would have liked to have known that you were aware of what was going on. That's all." Peter was rubbing the palms of his hands on his thighs trying to keep his eyes dry.

"Well, now you know. And I appreciate it." Dave sat back and straightened his shoulders. He was showing a side of himself that perhaps no one else in the office ever saw. Peter had never seen it before.

"You see Peter, when you want to do a job like mine, and you don't want to do it by the book, life gets complicated. You find yourself doing things that you didn't expect you would, things you wonder whether you ought to. I hope you at least get some comfort from the fact that I made considerations about you. I let you have a little more leash than I would have otherwise. I also tried to keep the pressure off you because I knew you'd find enough on your own. In a lot of ways I think you're a lot like me. I think you'd do my job similar to the way I do, not in all ways, but in some ways. At the same time I realize that you're a bit of a ditherer, and that it might take you longer than it would for most people."

"A ditherer? I guess you mean a ditherer with a temper."

Dave looked back out the window and seemed to be staring off into the distance. The ash on his cigarette got to be about an inch long, and it seemed as though he hadn't noticed, but just before it fell into his lap he flicked it into the ashtray and took a drag. A cloud of smoke rose around his face as he turned and stubbed it out.

"You know, Horace worked for me for about eleven years

and I really wanted to get rid of him until you started." He turned back to the window and continued. "That was your first job, if you remember, assisting him. Although you ended up doing most of the work from the start. You didn't know it at the time. You didn't know what was going on at all. When I thought you had safely developed the habit I moved you away to do other things. So it's not even really fair to say I gave you a lot of freedom, but I'll say it anyway. I just couldn't get rid of him. I couldn't find it in me. I assumed that something would happen eventually. So did you, I imagine. Perhaps we both killed him."

A faint horror broke out across Peter's chest. He felt he was being challenged to admit to something he never, until now, considered himself to be a part of. What actually were his intentions when he threw those papers back at Horace the other day?

"What do you mean?" Peter asked, struggling to keep his composure.

"You did march out of here like a storm trooper. I knew something was up. But, hey. This is our secret."

Peter sat ruminating over his possible guilt for some time until he decided that it was ridiculous to go on this way. He wasn't guilty of a thing, and he had to prove it to himself. At once he felt more confident. It was quite natural, this confusion. He got up and walked over to Horace's cubicle, but as he approached, it got harder for him to move. Standing about ten feet away he could almost hear the space humming. It seemed there was something there, but nothing more than a confusion, an electric field the dead man left behind.

Thank you Horace. This is what you left me in your will. Didn't you know that I had enough of my own. When Peter thought this the confusion seemed to stop and become pure presence for a moment. He felt he was being watched, not by a person, or even a ghost, but by a witless malice. Yet it was something inanimate, something that came not from a personality, but from decomposition. It vibrated on a similar wavelength to that thing inside him that made him want to reach out suddenly and break somebody's neck, not out of anger especially, but out of a desire to destroy. There were times, very often his happiest and most affectionate moments with Sally, that he suddenly felt he had wanted to tear her to pieces.

At times it seemed he was possessed by something very bad indeed. Otherwise he had no reason to believe in anything. If Horace was his first victim, there would be more.

He entered the space and sat down in Horace's chair. Whatever it was couldn't hurt him any more than he could hurt himself. It was probably his anyway, whatever it was, something he contaminated Horace with a few days ago, just a trace of his own evil energy. He took a manila envelope filled it with the piles of yellow pages lying on the desk. In his hands they felt like his own. Clear away the evidence.

When Peter got home he found Frank posing in front of a large mirror with his guitar. Loud staticky guitar chords played over the stereo while Frank lunged and twirled kung fu style, sometimes flailing the guitar recklessly around like an exotic medieval weapon. Peter ducked out of the way of the solid body just before it struck him in the head, and stumbled noisily into the wall.

"Oops. Sorry. I didn't hear you come in," Frank said, and walked over to the stereo to turn it down.

"I thought you saw me."

Frank grunted in the negative and laid his guitar down on the bed and sat down beside it. "So, what do you think?"

"What, was that supposed to be your stage show?"

"No, the music, man. This is my band." He went over and turned up the volume again. After a few seconds he turned it off.

"Interesting. Kind of like Ivory's band."

"Yeah. We work together a lot. By the way, I think she likes you. You should give her a call."

"Me? I don't think so." Peter went into his room and began to undress. "So what was that you were doing when I walked in, is that part of the performance?"

"No way. Are you kidding? It just makes me feel more comfortable with my instrument. I like to dance with it, and get weird with it. It's like going on the war path. First you have to do a war dance, get in touch with the duende in you. Or else you sound silly like everybody else."

"Oh." Peter realized he was getting used to this. What a pair they made. He lay down and stared at the ceiling, and called to Frank, "Hey, you can put that back on if you want." He heard some fumbling from the other room and then the music again. Relaxing, he heard Frank's guitar spiraling through his head, pleasantly infuriating, as he explored about through the cracks and water marks above. They mapped some sort of spatial-temporal zone, almost recognizable, though not anything he could remember, except for the fact he'd been staring at it for nearly two years now. The music ran through the patterns like water in a knotted canal. Around the perimeter of his room a low hum was slowly pulsing, making it infinitesimally brighter and darker. A migraine was possibly coming on. He focused on the squeaky little pink and yellow lights on his eyelids when he closed them. When they turned red and white he'd open his eyes, just before the pain would come. But tonight they faded to rust and grey, and he rode them out into rivulets of semi-sleep, hoping to run them down before their impressions began to set. Frightened forms were hiding in the cul de sacs of the in-betweens and around-backs. They were everywhere, born and dead in an instant, with their absurd architecture and contorted faces, some with long pointed teeth that used to frighten him when he was a child. He would lie awake hour after hour with his heart beating adrenaline into his small head, bleating and praying, knowing it was too late, that he had already committed the unforgivable crime of calling on these shapes to begin with. Lost, breathing irregularly as the coils of ectoplasm wove about his legs and arms, pulling them taught against his body straight and firm so that he couldn't move until he shook himself out of sleep. Then he'd lie awake for hours praying until he gave up. It was only a bad dream. Nothing to fear, he'd say over and over. In the other room was the television, the refrigerator. Home comforts and familiarity. Mother and father. His brother Dennis fast asleep. Snoring...

He remembered how his father's snoring used to scare him out of his mind, mostly after he had been drinking, deep into the morning when the rhythm suddenly changed, echoing and slithering over the walls and ceiling after him, hovering over his bed and giving voice to the monsters who swam the dark abomination. He was a bad boy, a very bad boy, and it was the badness that had come to take him, mangle and torture him. In the morning he'd be dead and his body full of sores and burns, his cock shredded and held together with pins for all his masturbation, dreaming of girls, molesting pure naked skin without a trace of sin or blemish until polluted unknowingly by the selfish and acidic cloud he sent: his secret spell of hate and desire.

Frank's guitar solo wormed through him like molten lead. All the threat of fantasy, long gone though reverberating from time to time in hours of insomnia, came back with an abrupt shrillness as he thought of Horace. He rose trembling, feeling silly and ashamed. Last time he had really fallen into that horrid spell he'd walked around like a zombie for a month and had all but lost his job. That's when Dave had rescued him, kept him busy. Sally had broken up with him and he had been hearing voices again.

He at last found comfort in remembering the warmth he had felt for Horace. Horace, the quietly cheerful graying and grisly ape in the adjacent cubicle, who would appear as if by magic, without a sound, with a confused and pleading smile, holding out pages with a pointing finger. It was almost a service to Peter he was providing by extending his ignorance and helplessness in such a way as to let another who is helpless help.

But Peter couldn't have been responsible for his death, because he had made too many efforts to save the old man. Only a basically good person would have rescued him as often as he did, making so many efforts, and coming to his defense when others would mock him. Once Horace had surrendered to his fully imagined obsolescence, he had become an opportunity for Peter to care for another person in a way that was different from any relationship he had in his entire life.

If it weren't for the fact that Frank was in the other room, just around the corner from his open door, he would have let himself cry. He hadn't cried, in fact, for all the weeks Frank had been with him. But his eyes wetted unnoticeably, and his chest rose heavily, falling slowly to the music of loss.

From behind the music came the resolute chirping of the telephone. He heard Frank answer it and rush out the door. A minute or two later a woman's voice followed him back in. He instantly recognized it as Ivory's. He crept off his bed and pushed the door closed slowly, trying not to be noticed, and began putting his pants on, but before he could get the second leg in, the door swung open wide.

"Hey Pete, look who's here." Frank and Ivory both stood smiling in the doorway.

He swung his upper body around. "Just a moment." Lurching around he slipped on the other leg almost tripping. When he had pulled them up he noticed that they were on backwards, so he took them off and, this time not trying to hide, put them back on as they watched. He looked up at Ivory and blushed.

"Aw. Is Petey embarrassed because the pretty girl caught him with his pants down," said Frank. "Maybe you should leave them off. You could be more useful to her that way." They both laughed, and Ivory's eyes probed his.

He looked down at the mass of flesh hanging over his belt and tried to cover it with a lanky arm as he rummaged his room for a tee shirt. He found a throwaway, something his mother had given him with a big "I'D RATHER BE SKINNY DIPPING" written across it and put it on.

"Come on man. We're going to get something to eat. Get your shoes on," said Frank.

He stood for a moment scratching his cheek. "But I'm supposed to call Sally. I gotta see what she's doing."

"No you're not. It's Tuesday. Remember? She's at acting class, or at dance class, or whatever she does. She won't be home 'til after ten. I've been keeping track for you."

"Oh. Okay." Having other people knowing what was going on in his life was making him feel vulnerable. "But I really wanted to eat in and save some money tonight."

"And eat what?" Frank went over to the refrigerator and opened the door. "Let's see. We have a jar of pickles, leftover Chinese food from a month ago. I see what you mean. I wouldn't want to miss out on that."

Peter put on his boots and a snap-button western shirt he found in his closet, and put it on over his tee shirt. It smelled of mildew, but it was all he could find at such short notice since almost everything else he had was in the laundry bag. In the mirror the shirt pulled and bunched over his mid-section where the snaps met. He tried sucking it in but realized that he wouldn't be able to hold it like that all night. Better just to let it be. He looked around for something else to wear, even through his laundry. Everything smelled a bit too ripe to wear out to dinner, so he decided to live with it.

"Hey cowboy. You ready yet?"

"Where we going?"

"The Ra Bar. How about it? Sound good to you?"

Peter was unaware that they served food there. But Frank assured him that they were only stopping there for a fast drink. He had to give the bartender a tape, the tape that they had been listening to. It was sort of an audition. The bartender would pass it on to the manager. If he liked it his band would get a short spot, and maybe more gigs following that.

"It's a great place to play, even though it's small and the crowd is a little rowdy. They mostly have male strippers and drag queens playing there, but not all the time. I think what we do is revolting enough."

"I think so." Ivory perked up after remaining silent for some time. "People will come in off the street if they like what they hear. I played there a few times and it went over well. Of course that's when I was going through my g-string and tinsel nipples stage. Maybe you should consider playing in your underwear."

The place was fairly crowded for as early as it was. People were scuttling back and forth in the narrow space, enjoying themselves. It didn't seem as creepy as Peter had always made it out to be. He'd only passed by on numerous occasions, dodging the leather and spiked mohawks jangling with chains and riveted with gladiator studs. Usually he would avoid places he imagined he could get brutally maimed, but this now resembled a fashion show more than it did the Roman coliseum, more of a Disney World reproduction of Conan The Barbarian Land. And for a show place the beer was cheap.

Frank tapped him on the shoulder and passed by, saying, "Why don't you sit down and have a drink. We'll only be a couple of minutes." Ivory followed him toward the back, and they both disappeared behind a door.

Once his support party was gone, a little of his initial comfort had begun to be invaded by odd twinges of vulnerability. Where he once felt like an explorer in a bevy of freakishness, he now was beginning to feel a little freakish himself. He stood gazing about, rocking back and forth to let people get by, deciding that perhaps a beer, or rather the act of purchasing a beer, would be a positive point in assimilating.

"Well if it isn't the straight-WHITEMAN, of Gutter Never Land!" It was a familiar voice and face where only the back of a head had been a moment ago. He was pulling an old knapsack off a stool beside him. "Let me buy you a beer, old sport." Peter directed his unfocused gawking toward Alex.

"Hi. What are you doing here?"

"The same thing you're doing. I told Frank to meet me here. I knew he had some business to do, and this place is as good as any. Here, sit down. I just made some room for you. Hurry up before that queen standing behind you grabs it. She's been eyeing it for some time."

Peter followed his directions and mounted his seat with

slow somnambulistic movements, as Alex ordered him a beer and went on talking.

"I want you to try some of this rat poison they call 'Tell Your Truth Ale.' It's made by a bunch of Iroquois's upstate. Hard to get, but I think it's a failure to be totally honest with you. Long before the micro-brewery thing hit they were making it for themselves, probably for about five cents a bottle. It's the kind of thing that goes over in a place like this."

The beers arrived with a double clump on the bar before them and Alex's mouth stretched into a seedy grin. "Go on. Take a swig."

Peter did, and its oily bitter taste set off a mild gag reaction as he swallowed.

"There you go. Takes some getting used to, sure. It's a *required* taste." He laughed.

"Tastes like chemical waste," said Peter, still warming up to both the brew and his company.

Alex grew serious. "You know what your trouble is, you don't love enough. There's nothing that you love enough. That's why you keep drifting away, back into yourself, into the quiet little dungeon inside your head."

This made Peter flinch. But he protested. "What the hell... There you go again," he wagged his head in disbelief. "You don't know me. Where do you come off . . . "

"Calm down. It's not as though I'm trying to be critical. I'm just trying to help. When you see somebody suffering, you wanna help."

"Yeah, well, not to seem ungrateful, but if I wanted a

shrink I'd order one." He settled for a moment and thought for a comeback. "I do love. In fact I'm very in love with a woman. Painfully so."

"Painfully. Okay. Maybe you are, but that's not what I mean. I'm not talking 'in love,' I'm talking 'love.' That's quite different."

"Oh, you mean like love your neighbor? All that hippy garbage we've been getting on the radio for the last twenty years?"

"No. Not that either. I mean simple love, the kind of love that could pull you out of yourself. Love drinking your beer. Love being here amidst all of these crazy queens. That's what I mean. I bet you half the time you're with that girlfriend of yours you're so uncomfortable trying to live up to what you think she thinks you should be that you don't even enjoy yourself."

Peter looked around the bar. It had been about three minutes since Frank and Ivory left him. He was growing a little impatient.

"See what I mean. You're getting restless. You want to get out of here. You can't even enjoy my company, or something as undemanding as that beer you've been slugging."

"This beer is disgusting!" He said it loud, and for a moment the whole place seemed to get silent except for a couple of snickers behind his back.

The barmaid strode up to him and said, "Is there any problem?"

"No, no. My friend's just a little aggravated. It's my fault. I've been instigating," Alex said.

She smiled, looked at Peter and wiped down the bar in front of them. He felt his face grow purple and covered it with his hand.

"That was better. See, you can come alive sometimes. It suits you more. Now tell me this. Is it true that you can't enjoy your beer, just the fun of it, because it tastes so bad? For me that's certainly a pleasure. I know something better'll come along. I'm not afraid it won't."

"Think about it, Peter."

A huge nest of hair haloed Peter's head from behind him. In the mirror he saw it, and it felt like it could be his own. He was half way between hypno-gorgeous and vertigo.

"Think about it Peter," Alex repeated.

He was wordless. The freak-shrink's voice floated breeze-like above the traffic jam in the tunnel. Everybody was going everywhere, but it was so slow it was almost backwards. He felt very thirsty, and took another drink.

"Peter, are you listening to me?"

He couldn't help thinking there was something dead in his bottle, maybe death itself. It had come back around to him, and now everyone was conspiring to get him back for what he did to Horace, but this knowledge aroused in him some powerfully defiant energy that had lay waiting for such a moment. He recognized it as an old friend and nodded to it. All he had to do was to crack the cipher. There was a system to the game they were all playing, and he could turn it around. The secret was in the true name of the beer. He drank, and he drank, and ordered another, and another, as Alex looked on rapturously, each sip bringing him a new descriptive term.

Detergent. CastorOil. Acetylene. Octopiss. Gangrenadeine. All it took was for him to project himself to the edge of his nerves and think like two live wires coming together. Old Motown hits were playing through the commotion, and he couldn't hear the words, only fragments and broken syllables. Babbeeyabalowyagaaa... Penicillininyacokacolaya. All the commotion in the place aligned itself to his cause.

Gabadoobadoobooda. Everybody was singing about the beer, all celebrating in utter disbelief its toxic savoir. Did somebody slip a tootsie roll in Peter's drink? Oh no. It's only Peter unwinding from a bad day. Zing! Oops, out flies the coiled spring-steel of his inner sanctum. The real pressure isn't getting work done. It never was. It's holding this impossibly small kernel of time between mitts of grey matter so what you say won't shock people when you start talking backwards, sideways, inside out, out your ass. And besides, god was always seeking revenge because he was a cheesy dresser, the whole world is at a ridiculous infantile state about to get sucked back into lifeless matter.

It's the head trips, and Peter had just ceased to let it go on any longer. Sorry Alex-old-pal, I've got an appointment with the chachayolotti man. He's come to deflate my tires and crank me up on the hoist for a change of air. Na na na.

"So don't you agree with me?" Erhoh... Interference coming in from a port locale. Dingdingding.

"Huh?"

"Exactly what I mean."

Exacalacalacky. Wachumoannnn. Hurry. Man the harpoon. SHFIFFFFFT!! Gotcha.

Peter dropped off of his seat and was out the door. All he knew was he had to hide. Quick! Overhere overhere. Across the street was a man with a crewed head and full beard handing out little black and white comic books. Cool.

"Jesus loves you."

"I love my beer."

The man looked angry, but his voice remained calm. "That's all right. Jesus will forgive you if you ask him to."

"Who the hell is he? I'm still trying to get away from Alex." Peter looked quickly from side to side. "D'you see'um?"

Then the man's eyes opened wide. "Hey. I know who you are. You're... you're... Peter Sturmer. We went to high..."

"Know what juniper is?"

"...school together. Remember..."

"I think they used it instead of hops."

"...me? I'm Larry Trun..."

"Makes you an easy target."

"...dell."

They found him four hours later in a dumpster by a construction site. Frank, Alex, and Ivory were joined by Larry. Peter had calmed down considerably by this time, and was wondering what it was that got him into this position. But he was fairly comfortable where he was, having found a few pieces of sheet rock broken auspiciously to the shape of his crooked spine, so until he could figure out what to do next, he decided to remain there and think about his situation. He knew they were coming. He could hear them all the way down the block, and tasted every second until... It was Alex's head he first saw dangling over the rim.

"Oh shit. Here he is."

Then Frank. "Okay Tarzan, it's time to go home. We've been looking all over for you." Peter let him take his hand and help him climb out.

"This is your old friend Larry. Larry Tumbrel," said Frank.

"Trundell."

"Right. We saw him standing across the street, staring at us when we walked out of the bar, so we asked him if he'd seen anyone that fit your description and sure enough."

"Yeah. I was kinda worried. You seemed like you were in some kind of trouble." He stood staring quizzically at Peter.

"Look, I called Sally. She's back at the apartment. We better go back," Frank said.

They all turned and walked back up the street. Peter followed, and Frank fell back next to him.

"She told me that there was some trouble with a guy at work, and that you were worried about him. Evidently she had gotten a call from your boss. She didn't know how he got her number, but she thought that he looked it up on your rolodex when you were out to lunch. He said to keep an eye on you, that the guy had died, and you weren't dealing with it too well."

A gush rose up into Peter's chest and suddenly he was crying. He listened to himself as the spasms cracked in his throat, carrying short bursts of falsetto into the cool evening air. Soon he was rattling like a baby, hunched over without control, and falling to his knees. Frank bent over and Peter could feel hands on his shoulders, rising and falling as his body shook. He didn't feel as though he was crying for any reason. It was just something his body wanted to do, going off like a child running in circles. Waves went through him in pleasing convulsions, although there was something ultimately hopeless and disparaging at bottom, and now he remembered. He was a killer.

He tried to tell Frank this. The others were there too, looking down over him in a semi-circle. No one would believe him. They knew nothing of it, and couldn't imagine what he was talking about. It was wickedly discouraging for him to be making his confession and to have everyone deny it, for he needed to reveal his guilt. He needed the release. It was like a lead ball in the middle of him pulling everything into collapsed nothingness.

Sure, it was a heart attack. How can you say you're responsible, they'd say, but Peter knew. He understood how a million little events could add up. A frown here, an unkind word there, all well timed. He sent out his bad energy, his wishes. There was no sense in pretending it didn't happen. The man was about to be buried. A weak person. A helpless person. An easy target.

The crying went on as they walked, but subsided before they made it back to the apartment. Before long he was stiff with fear and his hands were shaking. The killer could easily take over and go after his friends. It was near the surface, and even though it seemed under control, it made him terribly uneasy. Like an irresistible urge to urinate, it became more than just a battle with a sphincter, more a loop-de-loop of will, a strong force against another, but aren't they really the same? The two Peters were having a horrible disagreement. Frank, next to him, wasn't such an easy target, but Alex was. He could take out his keys, run up behind him, and jab them into his eyes. Frank would try to rescue him, but if he waited until they passed a trash can, he could surely find a bottle to break, take them all by surprise. It would be especially satisfying to kill Ivory. Watch the life drain from the pretty girl's eyes. He would go home all bloodied. Larry's holy tongue in his hand. Sally would be his last victim. His final mortification. With her he could yank out his own heart, remain bellowing until his own last breaths. Run headlong into shower fixtures until he'd beaten himself into an impossible mess. Yes, this is what he wanted. No.

No denying, the thoughts turned him on. He had been swallowing them for quite some time and now they were belching out in jagged little curlicues. It was time to fess up, at least to himself if he was the only one listening. Perhaps he was... only possessed? That would mean there was hope. No. It's been going on too long. Maybe there had been a time when he could have been saved, but that was before this happened. It had taken root. His own fault.

Peter was readying himself, frightened as he was. His hands were tightening into fists, and he was looking around for any sharp or heavy objects he could find. Something that could be used as a weapon. Little by little he was falling into a deep slouch, hovering in the shadows, arms dangling low at his sides, doubling over in fury.

Frank noticed Peter was drifting back and called over to him. "Hey what are you doing back there? You look like a fucking monkey."

Just then Peter made his break. He ran raving at Frank with all of his strength. He would tackle him and bite a big chunk out of his throat. He was almost at him when he slipped on a soft goo. For a moment he was flying, but his legs were too far above his head. He couldn't control it. Then the concrete was coming toward him at a tremendous speed.

The thud made his head vibrate like an aluminum pole he struck with the palm of his hand. Then the pain came. His arms, his knees, and especially... Ooowww my head!

Peter was crying hysterically again, slumped over in a little ball on the ground. Everyone stopped and turned around, and Frank stooped to grab his arm. Peter felt his body being pulled upward and gave in to it, pushing as hard as he could with his legs to get up.

"There you go," said Frank. "Now, what was that all about?"

Peter returned a sniffle and a whine, neither of which could be translated in his own mind. What happened a few moments ago seemed to be engulfed by an impenetrable vault, around which floated ghosts of past and present. Future was illegible. It smoldered ahead of him, releasing nothing. Smoke enveloped smoke, enveloped smoke. His head glowed with pain, and his knees and elbows radiated beneath the bloody spots of his jeans and shirt.

When Sally saw him, she stood for a while with the color gone from her face before saying anything. Then she suddenly demanded Peter take off his clothes at once. She filled the bath part way with cold water and dumped his pants and shirt in when he handed them to her. The others were in the other room talking quietly. Sally didn't say a word, but dropped the toilet seat and made Peter sit down. She inspected the scrapes, soaked a washcloth in hot water and peroxide, and began cleaning his wounds. Under the light she noticed the swelling blue knoll on his forehead, and called out, "Hey Frank, you guys keep any ice in the freezer?"

In a couple of seconds he was at the door. "No, I don't believe that we do. I don't really have any use for it, and neither does he, I would imagine."

"Then why don't you go out and get me some, will you? Here."

She reached out and handed him a couple of dollars.

"Sure."

There were voices and then footsteps of people leaving the apartment. When Sally swung the door open Ivory remained sitting on Frank's bed looking back with quiet interest. Peter sat dull-eyed against the throne. Sally squinted curiously, asking, "Where did you find him?"

"In a dumpster over on Seventh Street."

"What was he doing?"

"Nothing, as far as I could tell. Just sitting quietly."

"I was counting to forty over and over again," Peter broke in, to their surprise. "I usually count to ten when I can't get to sleep, but I was too wide awake. I wanted to go back to sleep so that it would be nice in the morning." His expression didn't change.

"Is there anything I could do?" Ivory asked Sally.

"I don't think so. Why don't you get some rest. You've had a hard evening. I'm sorry . . ."

"That's okay. Anything for Peter," said Ivory, as she collected her things. She gave Sally an enigmatic smirk and left.

Peter was taking this all in, but he was having trouble processing it. He tried to think of something to say, aware of how unsettling this must be for everybody. But nothing would come. Halfway through an idea, he would become distracted with the beginning of another. Nothing made sense. He was lucid enough to realize that. Although his body kept reminding him of what had happened, he was calm, yet unclear.

His body. Between the thunderous relapses of his throbbing head it would feel numb and dull. He wanted to talk to Sally, assure her that everything was all right, that no, he didn't need to go to the hospital. Everything was fine. He couldn't talk to her but perhaps his body could, and it wanted to. When she began soaking his knees again, he put his hand on her back, running it up and down her rib cage.

The experience of having Sally wash the blood off of his knees and cleaning his sores was sublime. He wanted more. Her hands were aflame with his blood. He watched them working hoping that they would work their way up his thighs. The slow way she worked seemed to show she was distracted. Could it be that the blood had aroused her in the same way? It was a new kind of sex, of making the connection without involving the usual organs, a way of touching and sensation arising between two people in this unexpected way that constructed a weak, but wholly present circuit, and he felt the tingle of it up his legs and into his head and hands. Without hesitation he swung his arms and tried to lift her up on his lap. At first she hesitated, almost pulling back, but then let herself float upward to her new position. Almost immediately Peter began kissing her, letting his hands glide over her torso. Sally sat impassive, staring down onto the bathroom tiles. Peter wanted to ask why but was having trouble forming the words. The ache had dulled, but the dullness seemed to spread deeper than even the pain had.

A moment later she retreated and put her hand on his cheek, looking deeply into his eyes, but backed off when he raised his hand to touch hers. What kind of animal play was this. But Sally was far from playing. He could tell from her eyes, which seemed puffy, almost infected with the opposite of possibility. He wanted to quell what he thought was her despair, but still, he couldn't speak. No words would come to him, almost as if the shock of banging his head against the street had erased something, or dislodged a required mechanism. There was nothing to say, no nervous banter. No making up anything now. It was a hum, a dead line. Empty, no worry. No care. No worry Sally, no worry. But she couldn't hear his thoughts. She still had the need of his thoughts, even though he needed nothing. Not even his body.

10

"Peter, Peter, Peter, come into my office. I need to speak with you right away." Dave was excited. His coffee splashed leaving trails flying out of his paper cup behind him as he dashed to his office.

Peter was numb and tired. He had spent most of the morning decorating his graphs and talking to Horace. He thought that if he could at least create a strong impression in the air, the man would go or at least leave him in peace. It seemed to work. No more buzzing, and no more cadaverous breezes floating through unexpectedly.

One more cup of coffee. That could do the trick. It wouldn't last long, but maybe one more after that, and then another.

Stay away, Horace. Stayaway stayaway. I didn't mean it. I didn't kill you. I'm done thinking that. No way no how did I ever have anything to do with it.

"Pete, I feel like the work you've been doing has just about come to an end. But don't worry. It's just that we're doing a bit of consolidating. There's no need for the kind of research you've been doing for now, so I was thinking, how'd you like to try something completely different, something new, in a completely different area of the firm? I think it would be something you'd be very good at." Dave shifted in his chair uneasily. "Management wants people who scan the mainframe for the remnants of ancient programs that were supposed to be disabled years ago and may still be getting executed somehow, ghost executables, if you like. They might be messing up files and taking up system time, slowing down normal processing. There's software that's supposed to be tracking them, but it seems not to be functioning very well and they actually need a body to go in there and snoop around. It seems a lot of this stuff got installed in a much older environment, somehow continues to wake up, and outside the scope of all the current monitoring systems. No one seems to know how this could possibly be, it's just that a lot of strange stuff has been happening to the data, and there's no explanation for some other things that have been happening as well. They don't need anyone with heavy high tech or programming skills, just good debuggers, and people with an out-of-left field approach. So, naturally, I thought of you, you weirdo. It's a good thing, since it might actually help save your job."

Peter felt his face buckle. He scratched the back of his neck.

"Don't go into shock about it. I don't think it's a permanent situation, but it's out of my control right now. We're all watching the courts, you know." He sat back and took another shaky sip from his cup. "You know I don't think it's ethical to go pulling people's coverage, but the whole industry's at stake. A lot of jobs are at stake. We're in the midst of a huge dilemma." He leaned over on his desk folding his hands over his nose, and looked out of the window.

"Dave, I hope you don't mind me asking you this," Peter began, "but why didn't you ever go into the movies?"

Dave tilted his head around and seemed to bond retinas

147

with Peter. "I'm serious." He was. "I'm very serious. Don't clown with me just now. This is important."

But there was something majestic and Aryan about Dave at this point. Strains of Lowengren seemed to mist off of his auburn locks. I'm serious too. I'm serious too, thought Peter, rising in his seat. You were never meant for insurance. Neither was I. I see you in Viking movies. You've got the character. You've got the looks. What do I have? I can't think. My head's still a little swollen.

"Do you understand me?"

Peter thought of his most acquiescent and comprehending look. Was he doing it? It was hard to tell. There was no mirror, only Dave. And he was reflecting only himself.

"Yes, of course. We always understand each other. Don't we?" Dave continued.

There was a turn of the head in the mirror. Then a returned glance out of the side of his left eye. Suspicious maybe, but conciliatory. "Okay then. You're to set up a meeting with this gal." Dave rose from his seat and walked over to Peter, handing him a business card. "I've already spoken to her, and have told her all about you. You're still reporting to me, but she will be sort of borrowing you. For now." The card belonged to a Michelle Blanchard, V.P. of the IS Security Council. Gulp. A new person with unmapped expectations and unknown quirks. Someone like his mother, possibly, always hovering over him with some kitchen tool or other.

When he made the call, Blanchard's secretary informed Peter that she was about to leave on vacation, and wouldn't have time to speak with him. But she had prepared a folder of instructions to help him get started, which was somewhat assuring. Once he actually got around to picking up and perusing the instructions, and later looked at the files, he rubbed his hands together, realizing it would take about two hours to complete the first set of tasks – actually all the work that had to be done by the end of next week. Which was excellent: more time to lunch on the pier and watch the gulls harass the tourists. He'd been much too busy lately, which was largely his own fault, he realized. It was hard for him to do anything, with his concentration waning. The image of Ivory stripping off the gray makeup from her pink skin always kept coming back to him like a chill breeze coming up through the middle of him. No one like that ever appealed to him before, no one with that hard edge, so it could not be appeal, though perhaps fascination with a mild revulsion. But was it really? Thinking about her infected him with an enticing nausea. It was odd perhaps after the previous night's encounter with Sally, Sally of the bloodstained hands. A memory that was hard for him to connect to now, in the daylight, the fluorescent office, an experience seemingly tied up in the night, a more deeply complicated knot of himself.

He logged onto the portfolio system, watching the phosphor-green columns of text trickle down upon the black and silent background, and perused, possibly for the last time, the list of stocks he had been responsible for monitoring. He felt they were almost his own. On the other hand, it was like peeping into a stranger's closet, where one came across, among the expected wools, tweeds, and button down shirts, uncanny things with strangely angled lapels, embarrassing plaids. There were the bank stocks, the airlines, auto makers and oil companies, but also European and Japanese stocks and bonds with strange names like the flavor of espresso beans chewed upon among cabbage leaves. Here they were only bits of sound and light – strange words perhaps with apparent connection to something produced – but on some other plane exploded into millions of people doing countless things, somehow meshing together into a confused fuzz of activity he couldn't even imagine. And all that activity somehow produced a stock price, relative to all other rows on the screen, and that's how these people decided what value was? It seemed doubtful. It was a huge truck rolling down a mountain road without a driver, people watching, hoping that their bets influenced the brakes and the steering apparatus, and this is what somehow drove the economy, kept people at work, safe, in homes and well fed. This is what kept them in and out of wars. And it was Peter who had been responsible for this particular list, as he was supposed to watch and report any unusual changes to the overall mess, but how would he even know?

He felt guilty, or moderately so, watched perhaps, yet he continued to scroll through until he reached the end. About twenty screens, each about fifteen to twenty lines long. This world he was leaving was the first step – where he was to begin his investigations, identifying wrongness, undesirable mutations in the data. This new role was going to be even easier than he thought, the mere appearance of actual productivity. Yet there was a numbness growing over the industry like a heavy blanket attempting to smother a small but resilient flame, a flame that could react chaotically, create unimaginable hazards, disasters, some of which might be due to the underbelly of the data, where he was going to be living from now on. He logged out of the system and decided to take off, maybe for an early lunch. His head was beginning to ache fiercely.

The sky was blue with only a few clouds so why did everything seem wrapped in a faint mist this late in the day? Maybe it was his head. It pulsed like a migraine, but it wasn't. It was the fall. Luckily the bump was hardly noticeable, but his knees felt like they might start bleeding through his pant legs any moment. Best not to bend them too quickly. Take your time. Don't walk so fast. Don't sit and stand so fast. Last night seemed far away, the recollections very dim. It spooked him to think about it for too long, always slipping into the same loop of questions, and though he found ways to distract himself, he continued sliding back to it anyway, curious as he was about what could possibly have gotten into him. It wasn't like he had been drunk. What, a couple of beers? There must have been something else. Strange that he didn't feel hung over.

Adrenaline. That's what it had to be. He was in a state of shock, and it just started pumping out. Not to worry. There must be other chemicals that the body will pump out at times like that. Endorphins? Toxic spinal fluids? Maybe he was having a flashback. That could explain a lot. Everything may have mixed together into a chaotic cocktail; every idea, every thought in his head, all that had been building up for some time, each matched with its equivalent biochemical compound, released suddenly and under pressure. Maybe the peak had come and gone. That thought he found somewhat comforting. Too many times in the recent past he had found himself at work in the morning wondering why he had acted the way he did the night before. These thoughts always arrived while at work. It was like his laboratory, safe and stabilizing. Outside it everything was beginning to seem a bit out of control. He didn't know how to act and he was doing stupid things because he was afraid.

At the pier he sat and began to wolf his sandwich down more out of anxious muscular relief, than of hunger. There was a warm damp wind blowing off the river and gray clouds took form over Brooklyn. From the north end of the walk a squirrel hobbled his way, but when it got closer it turned out to be a gull limping on a stump where its webbed foot had been torn away. The throbbing in Peter's head sunk into the bottom of his stomach. He felt sorry for the poor animal and tore off a piece of his lunch and offered it. The gull zig-zagged towards and away from him, studying him with one sarcastic bird eye, and kept on going. Peter threw the piece after it, but it paid no attention, just proceeded further toward the other end.

11

That evening walking home Peter noticed he had little recollection of how he spent the afternoon. This didn't disturb him because his memory was like that lately, very spotty, often riddled through with dream scraps, older memories cross-wired into his most current experiences as well as fantasy. He could remember sitting at his desk, doing something with the files, but not actually touching his keyboard. It was a purely visual memory, disembodied from physical sensation, but one that generated its own sensations of tension and lassitude.

The evening was warm. Sweat drenched his shirt and the seat of his pants. When he got home he should call Sally. She never returned his call today. Maybe she called when he was out to lunch. His body was stuck inside itself, though he had trouble feeling it fully. He could only feel a piece at a time. Sally was in a part that felt sad but tense, somewhere around his stomach. When he concentrated, waves of nausea ran through it. His body began walking very stiffly, as if he were afraid that someone was going to do him harm. Someone who was angry would get angry at him. Again, this was familiar. These are things he forgets, but then remembers when he's walking home. Trying to remember other things would make him feel dizzy. Sometimes it was better to try and not think at all, if he could only do it.

A car almost hit him as he began to cross Canal Street, but he jumped back in time almost falling into a woman with a large grocery bag. He turned around to apologize to the startled woman and other people moving away to avoid him. The light changed and he waited for all the cars to pass before going on, worried about being more of a nuisance. The air was unseasonably hot and close. Incendiary breezes blew out from under the cars. The sky had turned to cement and crushed the exhaust down onto his face. Was the air the same for everyone or was it registering only on him? His arms and legs were filled with lead, no, something liquid. Mercury. Mercury was poisonous, and so was everything in the air around him. He was poisonous. The others were poisonous. How long could they live this way? They could all be dying, unknowing, all being eaten away slowly from inside. Might as well keep drinking. Alcohol will at least rinse some of it out. When he got home he would drink a couple of scotches and pee silver.

He gazed about and looked for things that appeared silvery, mutable, hoping to find a correspondence in the world around him. There were car bumpers and mirrors, the glaze of light and images reflected in windows, all of which would slide across in a watery crawl imitating protozoa or droplets of immaterial substances leaking in from invisible worlds. And what might inhabit those worlds, but some demonic accountant of a heavenly IRS, keeping tabs on the very motoring around on two feet.

Sally, you're the only one who connects me with this time and space. I don't live until you're there. So much of this is nothing but a bad dream. None of this is real, not like the real I remember. Real was more crisp, like the lettuce out of grandfather's garden, the sound of that broken glass falling from the frame when I was renovating houses during the summers. Now you are the only thing. You make everything real. No hope until I feel you on my face. All comes and goes and comes and goes like phantoms across a cathode tube. Shadows of a distant TV show, one that's being aired in some remote neverland. No one knows what they're talking about. No one cares. Do you care when I say something? I don't care what these people care. So fucking miserable all of them. I feel like they want to kill me. Stupid straight white boy, what do you know? Go home to the suburbs. Climb a tree. Fuck you all. Love to climb a tree, but too old. Split my pants. This suit costs two hundred dollars. A cheap suit, but by my standards. Sally talk to me. Of course Peter I love you care what you say and listen to every word. So, where are you? I'm up in the ozone hollows where nobody has to care. The sun just shoots right through and burns away the skin and bones. Everything. I am sleeping dreaming and so are you, but you can't be aroused. Horace is here. He's not angry. He's only sad like you said he always was.

The church on Mott Street. Tall trees shade from the big almost blue leaves. Shadow almost unseen against the wall of orange brick. Dull silver sheen up above in nowhere. No more leaves, fallen like the rest of us. Back behind in time. Goodbye. Continue along sandwiched in gray pustules of sky and sidewalk, until Houston breaks. Out into the open again into danger and traffic. Under a rickety stack of postered scaffolding and onto the open road to the meridian where it's safe until the throng has passed.

As he passes the parking lot on Bleecker and Bowery he

sees a ragged man holding himself up by the chain linked fence. He is staring out at Peter and he is Horace. His eyes are glazed, too lost to be frightened. The same spittle's hanging from his lower lip, but more. His eyes call, Peter, Peter, I need you to help me out of this mess. I don't know what I'm here for. I don't know what I'm doing, I'm just very tired and I can't find a place to lie down. Take me back with you. Take me back to my wife. I need her, and I know she is very sad without me. But it's not Horace after all. It's another man; it could have been anyone. For a moment a ghost, but now he is following. Peter can't resist it, the invitation.

The door swings open without Peter turning the lock. On Frank's bed Ivory lays stretched out reading a magazine. Sax is playing over a string bass and piano on the stereo. Snare and cymbals. He looks about for a moment and notices they are alone. "Where's Frank?" asks the voice that seems to come from an adjacent body.

"He's got band business." She looks back down and rubs her finger along her eyebrow. "I thought I'd stick around to see if you wanted to have dinner."

"I was going to call Sally."

"Call her."

He goes directly to the phone without putting his book down and dials with an outstretched finger. It's shaking. It seems to be telling him that it doesn't want to touch the buttons. Before he hears the first ring he puts down the receiver. "Shit."

"What's the matter?"

"Wrong number."

"Oh."

He lifted it again and put it back down, sits down next to her and thumbs the pages of his book. There was a feeling of warming. His suit was damp with sweat from the walk, but now beads were forming on his forehead. On his other side the shade of Horace stood slouching with his droopy eyes and mouth, and this moved Peter closer to her. Something like a tear ran down his cheek, followed by a soft chuckle. Her finger. She sits up with a secret smile that makes him fall away distantly, no longer in control. The heat unsettled him so he stood up and walked across the room, realizing a sudden conflict. But it was too late because she stood up and grabbed his head, kissing him squarely, and they both fell back down, just sat there, arms entangling and then coming apart. It was too late for him and Sally, he began to sense, to fear. With an inexplicable immediacy he realized that this nearly unknown, perhaps unknowable person, this Ivory, or whatever her real name was, reached him in a way Sally could never do, and he could never approach with her. He kissed her once, and as soon as he did she pulled him down, and they just lay there for a while.

The sex wasn't like sex at all, not like two bodies fucking, but as if they had each both melted into a sticky substance that joined and warmed one another, intermingling at an almost molecular level. It was both healing and harming. Things were breaking up and rearranging themselves in a multiplicity of different ways. The swarm of images in Peter's head whorled and slid in and out of place in a kind of greater than three dimensional geometry that was unimaginable, though somehow perceivable in his present state. At one moment he was a gaseous planetary orb, and Ivory was both the smallest possible particle, penetrating as a seed of tremendous beyond-nuclear power, and at the same time the unlimited space around him. And within that space he also began to expand and sense something of a latent potential, not only of himself, but of ever minutia of cellular life and what it on its own was capable of. Another moment he was every living and dead thing in the universe, and was looking back at his pathetic, helpless self, the single body lost among billions, trying to find its way, alongside its twin, both incapable of using any of this most likely psychotic knowledge for anything but to let it slowly creep through them and burn everything he knew about himself away.

"Peter, I didn't know you cared!" said Frank as he closed and locked the door behind him. Peter turned around to see his long grin. He rolled away from Ivory and sat up.

"Really man, it's okay. Relax. Don't worry. We're all just friends here."

Peter let Ivory tackle him back across the bed, but remained passive as she kissed him on the side of the face. "I'm not supposed to be doing this. It's not good."

"Well brother, sometimes you don't have a choice. It wasn't up to you. I could tell the first time I saw you together."

"But Sally. I'm supposed to..." He was holding his head in his hand.

Ivory tugged his head back by the hair on the top of his head and pushed him away.

"I'd watch what you say, man," said Frank with chuckle. "You've maybe got somebody else's feelings to consider now."

Peter turned his head toward her and said, "I'm sorry. I don't know how this happened."

"Shit Peter, we were just snuggling."

"Yeah, but no, it wasn't just snuggling. And I didn't plan on it. I swear."

"I know you didn't. Nobody did. Bellamonia did. And you're having a typical male response. But don't you see? It's not like I wanted this either," said Ivory.

"What's going on? You're confusing me," said Peter without feeling, hypnotized with conflict.

"The Black Fire. You're in it. But don't fuck it up or it fucks with you. It burns everything down so you can start over."

"The what?" A chill that brought him back to attention.

"It's something she went through a while back," said Frank. "Changed her for life, and now it's changing you. That's what she calls it. Everybody calls it something different. It's like when your Bellamonia surges out of control. You're the only one she's met who is having it the more or less same way she did. You guys are stuck together. True love." There was something nearly sarcastic about his tone, but not quite.

"Bellamonia is love," said Ivory, "but not how you usually think of love, just like how gravity isn't really an attraction between objects, but the way they follow the curvature of space. Bellamonia is that kind of love, and the black fire is its raw, unpredictable form. It is Shakti and Shiva. It ain't Romeo and Juliette, it's the Surrealist, radioactive, maybe inhuman version. That's our love."

"Look, if you think this is going to go on, you're crazy. I'm in love with somebody else." But Peter knew it was over, that being with Sally had been a fantasy and a mismatch, more a constant source of frustration than a thing to celebrate, just like most things in his life that promised a kind of satisfaction that always eluded him.

Ivory looked over at Frank. Both faces were expressionless. She put her hand on Peter's shoulder and said, staring off into space, "You don't love her. She might mean something to you, but it's not good for you. You're only going to drive yourself crazy if you don't stop it. I'm your only chance." With that she pulled him closer. He didn't resist. Something in him always wanted to believe what he was told. He leaned over into her shoulder and a tear ran down his cheek. His life was over once again, with a new and unintelligible one burning him into resignation.

"But it's not going to be easy. I can be one hell of a bitch, and I think you already realize that. I'm telling you right now. In the long run you'll be better off. I can bring things out of you that she couldn't, but you might not like that either." For a moment her face hardened frightfully, leaving Peter strange and alone, but when she noticed she softened up, rubbing her hand over his chest.

"You know, I never liked hairy men. It's funny how quickly you can take to things in the right circumstances."

She patted him on his flabby stomach. The slappy clapping sound annoyed and embarrassed him. She was having fun with him, it was clear, and in the midst of ruining his life. There was no way in the world a woman like her could ever find him attractive. Horrified, he rolled over and stared at the door knob, imagining he could see his reflection. It was too old and worn. Horace, how about me? Can you help me? Out of this?

Ivory snuggled up behind him and draped her arm over his shoulder. "Don't worry. I'll take care of you. I know this is going to be difficult for you."

It must have been several minutes. Peter seemed to have dozed off, exhausted after all of the fervor. The phone rang, and before he could realize what it was, Frank had picked it up.

"Hi, Sally."

Peter reached his arm up, but Frank turned away from him.

"No, Peter's not here right now. I'll tell him you called. I gotta go. Someone's on the other line."

Peter sat up, and when Frank put down the receiver he reached for it. Frank grabbed his wrist and held it. "Are you sure you're ready for this?"

Peter was furious. He felt his fist tighten and he pulled his arm away.

"Come on man. Relax. Put your clothes on, and let's get something to eat. I don't think you should talk to her tonight."

They were on their way to *Catastrophe*. Peter's hand succumbed to Ivory's waist, as he abandoned himself to the tepid pleasures of the present, like a convict out on recreation. He knew he couldn't trust these people, and almost everyone who calls him a friend—namely Sally's friends—would surely not speak to him again. Now about to enter the Post

Peter Sturmer era. The murderer/adulterer felt himself collect grime, a greasy gray-brown snow that fell on him and him alone, gathering in his clothes and the cracks and lines of his face and hands. But there was something comforting in this, something he hadn't expected. They were right after all, for now he had fallen to his rightful spot, what he was born to be and never wanted to admit. It was terrifying, but at the moment he was too tired and he knew he'd never be able to fight it, that evil was winning. So be it.

He felt crinkly and awake. He felt Ivory's ribs between his fingers, and he felt closer to her than he had been to anyone for a long time. The world was now telling him to give in, to sink back into weakness like a big, soft, Lazy Boy Chair, maybe with nails coming up through the fabric. He went black with a delight that was the suicide of his despair. For a moment, maybe several, he knew the feeling of being completely in control of his life.

Iris approached them from further down the sidewalk. The surprise straightened Peter's spine, and he quickly took his arm from around Ivory's back, but not soon enough. She had already seen him. There was no way she couldn't have. It would have been better if he hadn't responded at all, but he had made it obvious with his guilty reaction. His hands were shaking when they met, which he tried to hide by clumsily introducing everyone.

"You haven't met my roommate have you?" he asked.

"No, but I've heard a lot about you." She smiled at Frank, but turned a strange look back to Peter. For a moment Peter thought it had less to do with him betraying her friend than herself. Peter knew he had set himself up as the male friend she could trust, but no more. An unspoken impression in the air made that clear."And this is Ivory. I don't think you've met."

"No."

As they both looked at each other, friendly, but firmly, Ivory placed her hand on Peter's shoulder blade and began stroking his back. Peter was jagged out on a chill that rocked him back and forth. He had to spread his feet in order to keep from falling over.

"Our Peter's been sick," said Ivory. "We're taking him out to make sure he eats something. Do you want to join us?"

"I'd love to, but I'm supposed to meet Sally back at your apartment," said Iris, looking back at Peter. "She told me to meet her there. She told me what happened last night. I'm surprised..."

"I went to work today," he said quietly, trying to hide the shakiness of his voice. "It's nothing. I'm just feeling a little dizzy. That's all." There was a short spell of paralysis in all of his muscles.

"I'm going back," he said with low voltage streaming over his tongue and cheeks. So this is it. To think just an hour ago . . .

"Well then, we'll all go back," Frank joined in, fully engaged. It was obvious that he was truly enjoying himself. Peter wanted to throw him through a storefront. Maybe it's time for him to be looking for a new apartment. Wait.

Sally had a look of pained confusion sitting amidst a room strewn with Peter's work clothes, some hanging off a bed with stained sheets, an obviously wrecked bed. Ivory's tampon still sat on the corner. Somehow it hadn't completely hit her.

Peter tried to keep Ivory on the opposite side of the room as he wandered around, but Iris seemed to be broadcasting something with her eyes in that peculiar way women have when they know each other inside out. Suddenly Sally's face grew tight in a way Peter had rarely seen before. He was readying himself for her onslaught, but when she looked at him her face was only vacant. Little by little it grew pale and tense until red picked up on the tops or her cheeks. She looked quickly around, grabbing her things clumsily, and flew out the door, slamming it behind her. Iris took off after her. Peter almost followed, but inertia caught him balancing on one foot. The FTD Florist man. No wings on his ankles, no red suit, just a stumbling bumpkin with nowhere to go and nothing to do.

It hadn't hit him yet. He wasn't sure it would, but everyone else was waiting. A couple of minutes went by before anyone said anything. Ivory put her hand on his back again. Frank stood with his arms crossed leaning against the table. He put his hands up in a gesture of disbelief. His face seemed moved, sullen, and something in that made Peter trust him again, if only long enough not to take the lamp off the table and beat his brains out. He needed them now, if only by default. For the time being he held to the exasperation necessary to face that. Tomorrow? Well tomorrow, he'd see about tomorrow.

He awoke to the feeling of lips pressing against his neck. There was an arm around him, which he at first thought was Sally's—though it was very similar to hers, it was smaller and thinner. His eyes opened and he realized he was in Frank's bed. The arm belonged to someone he thought of as a stranger. Oh, something did happen last night. Now he remembered. Not only had the accident happened, but it happened another two or three times afterwards. So much for appropriate behavior. So much for mourning over lost love. Yet it was sure to happen. He could remember. Long months of agonizing or feeling dead, waiting for Sally to come around. How could he ever imagine that he'd spit in her face once she did.

And what he felt now was the eerie delight he had felt when he sliced his hand open while shucking clams at a barbecue one summer evening. The blood poured down his arm like a cracked water main and he looked at it and felt something magical was about to happen. He could die from this, he thought. Time was spilling, much faster than usual.

Something did feel good about this, but he worried how it would turn out in the end. The end of what? The ends are all over. The stories are over. Something else was beginning that had no beginning, and it was squiggly lines that tangled and knotted and took off in opposite directions. It could be weeks before Sally would be willing to listen to him, months maybe, years, when their squiggly lines came back around. Then they would no longer form a heart. No more hearts for them. Just eyes, angry, and tear drop shapes. Someone else would come and marry her, have the children Peter could have had with her, but the ends are still to come for her. That's the main difference, that's why they're flying apart, not because of his crime. He no longer had to try so hard, although now he really was at the mercy of his whims.

12

When Peter got back to work he grabbed the picture of Sally in its plastic case and placed it face down on top of the monitor where it had been standing. And it hit him with an anxious gloom, something rather different from the downer love songs he had grown up with and their disquieted raptures that seemed almost more beautiful than the thing they presumed to mourn. It was more a dull horror sucking physically at his heart, but in a way that left him numb, almost apathetic to the cause.

He pulled the square of matches off of the cubicle wall, just hard enough so that an edge tore a slight bit, and leaned it up against the base of the plastic case. A little reminder of some overlooked capability of his, but what, and for what purpose? It brought no comfort now that he had just dove in and out of something and he couldn't see tomorrow, couldn't imagine any longer how it was going to be. It had been getting more like that, but now this void was cracked wide open. What after all was there but this space, and his own presence in it? So many memories, now warped, turned on themselves. And it dawned on him that his imagined future with Sally had defined him, set all expectations. He no longer knew who he was and what to do with himself.

He turned on the PC so that there was at least something. There was the sound of the drive cranking and the hum of the fan. Soon this moment too would be vague memory, one he wouldn't recall in detail and it made him feel lonely. The idea of Sally, the Sally-memory, was an imprint he had kept at hand to stave off emptiness and boredom. It helped him to decide, though it often mutated into something different from the flesh-and-blood Sally, the phone voice and bodily Sally. At times he'd have trouble figuring out which was more real, or at least more significant. Now nothing was real. Nothing was anything. His infrastructure was formless and veering to and fro. But things could change shape as much as they wanted for all he cared. His hair could turn into twigs and fall out. His batteries could fall out.

Peter wanted to think about Sally, but instead of her face he saw lined yellow pages with diagrams falling apart, flow charts whose flows dissembled and flailed aimlessly. Cartoon squirrels devoured stick figures reaching out to each other. Whole architectures had gone to the mud. No, Sally no longer existed in any way that was useful to the habit machinery, though it tried continuously to snap out familiar shapes based on past material. That Sally at the core of the mechanism was dead or demolished. Otherwise, everything was okay, he thought. Everything was fine. No bomb would go off, it seemed, only a burn. Wet fuse or faulty ignition, perhaps a neglect of planning on his part. One couldn't be sure. There could be a surprise attack, or one out of the sky, or out of his nervous ambling between dream and flat-line stare. How could one tell that nothing inside him, whether true and valid, or something that had crept or was flung into him, hadn't been up to mischief and that this whole debacle with Sally and Ivory wasn't about that to begin with? Something alien for which he was now doing reconnaissance. But what the fuck was it up to and what was it thinking? It had never occurred to him before, this being a lackey host for an unknown and uninvited entity, at least not until recently as he realized that he could never fully remember every minute of his day. Plenty of cracks where anyone could sneak in sneak out without him ever knowing it. A chill had him look through his drawers, opening each one and slamming them, finally forcing a smile at himself.

Maybe I didn't do it. Maybe I imagined all that with Ivory, and Sally never came over and never left, therefore. . .

The thought of calling her sent Peter's hand reaching for the phone, but it drew back in fear. He played back the recording in his head, remembering the sensations, testing them against things he knew had occurred without a doubt, and then tried to commune with that thing, whatever it was, he suspected was responsible. It knew better than he what had happened. It remembered better than he did the softness, warmth. He brought his hands to his face, closer to his brain.

Yes, I think I had sex with someone last night and I don't think it was Sally. It could have been Sally, but I don't remember it being Sally, and it doesn't seem like Sally. I remember it being Ivory.

As impossible as it seemed he did what she always said he'd do and warned him not to do. "Don't fuck me Peter!" she would say, meaning of course, don't fuck somebody else. It didn't seem to matter. It felt like she was in there too. And now everything had changed because he was fucking one body and not another. So many bodies. He could hardly keep track. *I might as well fuck or not fuck anybody I want. Not I want. What does I want have to do with it? I might as well fuck Frank. I might as well fuck me. I might as well fuck the fucking wall.*

Peter stared into the monitor, waiting for the genie to appear and tell him what to do. A voice was slowly becoming audible, similar to his own back-of-the-head voice, but with greater poise and sarcasm. Yes sir, what do we have here, my friend the elephant in the junk shop. Glassware down this way buddy. Here's a chandelier to catch in that outrageous mop of self-possession you owe yourself and its disintegration too. You might as well fuck me too, but watch the circuitry. It'll burn you to smithereens. Actually, I was thinking you ought to take a break from mating behavior for the time being. I know that you probably haven't had much for someone your age. It's a shame, but you never did learn how to make the proper place for it in your life. In fact consider giving it up all together. It's your best bet.

What are you talking about? I know I've just messed my life up, but I've got this hot babe waiting back at the pad for me. You're telling me to turn my nose up to that?

Listen I know what you're feeling. The truth is never easy to take. Especially in your case. But look Peter, you know she's psychotic. You said so yourself. It's only a matter of time before she snuffs out your candle or tears your heart out like every other encounter you've had in the reproductive rehearsal space. Besides, think about us. I know what's best for you. You'd be no fucking good if it wasn't for me. I do all your work for you. And you're still teetering. You haven't fallen yet.

Wait. Wait. Who the hell do I think I'm talking to?

What's the difference? I do the thinking from now on. You listen to me.

Peter turned it off and stared into his reflection in the blank screen. Every cubicle around him exuded rhythms of keyboard clicking, sighs, phones ringing off the hook. The reflection he saw of himself was cartoonish and distorted. A tiny man with toothpick arms hanging down beside him. Over his left eye and forehead, extending upwards like a huge feather was a thumb print. Is that you genie? I can't get rid of you, can I? At least I shut you up for the time being. Who needs to know what you have to say, truth, or no truth. He suddenly noticed another reflection behind his own. Until then he hadn't realized he'd been talking aloud. He spun around in his chair. "Horace, I'm telling you, get the fuck away from me."

It was Dave.

"Who are you talking to?"

"Who do you think? Myself, of course." The realization made his hands rattle on the keys.

"You called me Horace.'"

"I guess I was having an imaginary conversation. Just filling up the void he left."

"Hmm. . . Interesting. You almost seem to miss him, but you tell him to split. Is that the way you used to talk to him?"

"No, but I figure there's no sense in trying to spare him now, is there? He could be wandering around here right now, but as long as I don't have to look at that pitiful face I can say whatever I want, can't I?" Peter's voice had steadily risen in volume.

"Hey, hey, easy." Dave put his index finger against his lips.

The typing in the nearby work areas had ceased, but commenced after a few moments.

"Well, I just wanted to see how you were doing, but I guess you're still cranking yourself up for the next curve. In the middle of the 'mental shift,' as you say?" Peter angled his head and put up his hands in an 'I guess so,' gesture, and rebooted the PC.

"Okay, just let me know if we need to talk again," Dave said before taking off.

"Okay, but I think we're all good, at least for the moment."

For years, Peter was beginning to realize, he was functioning covertly. The work was different from what it appeared. There was an intriguing stream of material running almost unnoticed among his thoughts, and he wanted more than anything to have something to attach it to, rather than watch it run off into nothingness. It needed a focus, this stuff he was impregnated with, a way to make it concrete and send it out and around. Without that it was only going to get worse. Its isolation was getting the best of him, if it hadn't already. His personal life had become vacant. Having a new group of playmates seemed dangerous, but welcome. He just wished he had more in common with them. In some ways he did. Frank, Ivory and Alex all lived in their altered realities as much as he, although they seemed to do so with a deeper faith. Peter would get lost in his, but would always resurface out of mistrust. They lived in theirs, following their illusions in preposterous ways. It was cultish the way they carried on, and although he looked at them as rather foolish, he was envious. The closest he came was at particular moments when he was working, and a myriad of incremental changes would take place. The space around him would expand and glow. He was a mad metaphysician working out a tract of enormous power. Or perhaps a spy, picking up information about the way life went on within these walls and cubicles. He'd observe and catalog motivations, behaviors. He'd watch the others interact, pretend to care about the things they did in order to get further inside. Sooner or later he'd end up with only himself to spy on. There would be no alternative but to continue, and with no one to report back to. Nor could he escape from the habit of espionage, no way to forget or be forgotten. Life had begun to get dull and complex at the same time. There was no point to it. There had been Sally, that separate space, a haven from his own machinery.

He knew he couldn't go on being a spy for too much longer. It had been like this before, but never quite as extreme. Now it was like something he swallowed that was growing inside his chest, running up his spine into his head. The tension spreading upward from his neck made him feel as though it was going to explode. Getting himself to put his attention on his work was like pushing a loaded cart with his skull.

He booted the terminal again and waited. *Genie, Genie, talk to me again. I don't know if I want good advice or just a good argument. I'm lost. I don't know where my life is going and it usually seems as though I don't care. Should I care? Does it make any difference one way or another? There doesn't seem to be too much that I have an overwhelming fondness for. How the hell am I supposed to be motivated to be anything else but what I am, which is what? A fuck up. I just proved that. What should I do? I might get too old to do this job.*

It was well into the afternoon by the time he gained the courage to call Sally, but she said very little and refused to see him, and whatever few words he got out of her seemed to bore a hole into the center of his body. They were like the words of an irate stranger he'd accidentally done bodily damage to. It seemed the remaining life was sucked out by that phone call. He was at the cusp of tears but couldn't manage to work them out. Not even in the privacy of his own home. It was one of the things he dreaded about letting people in to share his space. In only a couple of months they had fully infested his life and he couldn't figure out if he was grateful or not. Everything was strange, blurred. He had trouble recognizing himself, who he was becoming. Only traces of his former self remained, haunting the uninhabited corners. A ghost of a ghost. Whose ghost? Horace perhaps? A face in the mirror took him by surprise before he could make it back into his own recognizable self. It caught him looking back at times and stood staring, waiting for recognition. Something he didn't know was inside with him, and it wanted him to know. The Peter he had known was suspended between an idea and the rootless awareness occupying his body. And what was this other thing?

The thought occupied him all the way home. Luckily, or not, there was nobody around when he arrived, just a note from Ivory, saying she was picking up things to make for dinner. Did she ever work? He didn't even know if she had a job, and very little else for that matter. He went into the bathroom and closed the door behind him and looked. Now that he knew what he was looking for, it was there. That strange face, his own, but with an expression he didn't feel he owned. Was it malice, or was it something else? A kind of knowing? It seemed to know something it wanted him to know, but stood back patiently and relaxed, waiting, as if it had forever.

Okay, what do you want? Nothing. No reply. Whoever it was used silence better than he could imagine using words. The frightened face appeared. It was the one Peter recognized as his own. Years ago his brother Dennis would stare into the mirror in the morning and pick the sleep out his eyes. It was the sandman, he would say. He could still see his face in his. He looked like Peter Pan and he was smiling. All those years ago, gone in a blink. Did Dennis still see anything in the mirror besides his own face? Peter doubted it. It was too bad, because it was one of the things he liked most about his brother. He'd stand behind him, a head higher, and listen as he spoke, wishing there was a place he could go behind the mirror. All the good things belonged to Dennis. He was the dreamy kid who'd have all the stories to tell. Everyone would listen. Grandmother would listen. Mom and Dad would worry and bring him to the shrink. They never understood. Peter got all his dreaming from Dennis and needed him for that. Now he had his own, an assortment of nightmares. Tears rolled down his cheeks and he turned on the cold water. A door slammed. He splashed water on his face and dried it on a towel, thinking, why does everyone want to kill me?

Sally stood behind the door when he opened it. In her arms were all of Peter's belongings that she had at her apartment. A couple of suits were crammed into a trash bag, along with some shoes, socks, and a pair of jeans. She put it down on the floor and dumped out a duffle-bag of books.

She turned back to him and said, "You're exactly right. I've been meaning for this to happen for some time. I couldn't live with it any longer, but I couldn't let go."

Peter looked at her stunned. "It was an accident. I swear. I think it had something to do with the knock on my head."

"No. Come on. You felt it."

"Felt what?"

"The last year. I tried to make it good. I tried to love you and give you every last piece, but it's obvious. You've been drifting away. I don't even think you know who I am anymore."

"What do you mean? I think I know you better."

"It's been getting lonely."

She sat down and stared at him. "I wish you'd see somebody. A doctor, or a shrink."

"What are you talking about?"

"You know, that night in there," she pointed toward the bathroom, "I felt like I was with someone I didn't even know. Some maniac. It's not like you hurt me or anything, but it's just the way you acted. Like an animal. It had nothing to do with us. Worse than that, it had nothing to do with being human." She turned her eyes away as if she was about to cry. "That's kind of the way it's been lately."

"But it seemed like things were getting better, just recently."

"I was pretending, hoping you'd come around, but this proves it."

A buzzing silence fell between them. Then she left. Gone like an off-duty cab in the last hours of the night. Peter sat down where she had been and felt the warmth she left, straining for moments before it became his. He sat with the image of her face fading, that beautiful glare. When it was gone for good he let the numbing fill him and dozed.

The sound of the door roused him. It was Frank and Ivory carrying bags of groceries. When they asked him how he was feeling he told them what had happened, and Frank decided it was time for action. He had talked Alex into lending them the van for the rest of the week in case a trip out of town was called for.

"Oh, typical, shit hits the fan and you wanna have a road trip. Sorry, I have to work. It's only Wednesday. If you really think this is a thing that needs to be done, can't we wait for the weekend?"

"Don't worry about it. Ivory will call in sick for you. We'll leave tonight, after dinner of course. But it's important that we get you out of the city at this point."

"But I've got too much to do. I can't play hooky just like that." Peter was panicking, and the others saw it.

"No way. You told us yesterday you'd have nothing to do until the beginning of next week when your new boss came back. Remember? You're not getting out of this one."

"Getting out of this one? Listen, I appreciate your concern, but why do you feel the need to do this? Why are you trying to be my big brother? You're years younger than me, first of all."

"Because no one else was. Alex has been making a study of you. He likes you, you know. He cares. He says, 'Keep an eye on that Peter. He's got some interesting hurdles he's crossing.' He thinks you're one of us."

"One of us? What does that mean? One of What?"

Frank looked puzzled for a moment, and then a smile broke across his face. "I don't know. Haven't been able to figure it out. I mean, your guess is as good as mine. But I trust he knows what he's talking about. He's usually right with people."

Peter dropped his head into his hands. His speech came muffled. "I'm not going."

"What?"

"I'm not going. I'm sorry, but you have no right to make these demands on me."

"Demands? This is for your own good. You need to get away. That's that."

"And what about you?" Peter turned to Ivory. "What do you think about all this?"

"I think he's right," she said. "You're about to go... Let's just say things are going to get a bit weird for you, weird like it's been, but maybe a bit further. You need to go where you can cause the least damage, trust me on this. I know you have no reason to. I just ruined your love life, after all." There was a wry smile on her face. "Don't worry. I'll be here waiting for you."

Secretly it was what he wanted to do, to flee suddenly, to fly out of a cannon into an ocean and swim across its entirety to some deserted spot. And this is what they knew, having taken it upon themselves to remove all the barriers between his senseless impulses and his behavior so that he could slip further into darkness. And in this way they were less than human, more like devices of his own destruction. Where there should have been panic he felt only the relaxation of his entire body, as if he had given up the fight, this time completely. He ran quickly to the bathroom and slammed the door, yanking his pants and sitting just in time to let go of everything that was inside of him in big angry bursts. It was then that the fear had come. He sat shivering on the bowl, expecting to die.

They had him. His head hung sullenly like butcher meat.

When he came out he wondered how he should prepare. It was a simple thing, playing hooky for a couple of days and taking a drive out of the city. He wasn't sure why his knees were rubbery, eyes a little out of focus. Everything was happening too fast. He hadn't called in sick in over two years, and never called in just to take a day off when he wanted it. It didn't seem honest.

Well Peter, he interrogated himself through the freeze of indecision. Yes. No. Yes. No. What is it?. "What can I do to start getting ready?" he asked Frank.

"Here," Frank said, pointing to a plastic bag full of greens, "wash some lettuce, but first wash your hands, will you? And then slice up some mushrooms. I'll open a bottle of wine."

"No, I mean for the trip. What should I do? What should I bring?"

"I don't know. Bring what you usually bring. A toothbrush. A change of underwear."

"Bring your ego," said Ivory, "so Frank can smash it up in an accident." She smiled gleefully at him, at his awareness of his discomfort.

"My ego? What do you mean? Me, an ego? I don't think I have an ego! Ho ho. That's funny." He paced back and forth nervously, feeling as though his weight was warping the boards beneath his feet.

13

The van smelled like pot smoke and gasoline. Peter was belching tomato sauce and vinegar as they sped up the windy FDR. Pink sun still streaked the windows on Roosevelt Island. It was about eight o'clock and the warm humid air blowing in over Peter's face had the taste of night in it. There was a barely detectable summer evening sensuality, almost a scent, he remembered from childhood running around backyards, sweating and laughing, discovering black magic in hide and seek shadows. Things he would forget: how twilight and evening were the most auspicious times for dogs and children, how energy ceased to inhibit itself as it found new hiding places, in shadows no longer limited to the spaces beneath the trees and eaves of houses, but cast about by the whole world. There was much you could forget when you were busy working and worrying about everything you had, and everything you were afraid to miss, and this drugginess of the most ordinary, which had become almost foreign to Peter, had begun seeping through the callus of those years, had him flashing back, and he felt, light as it still was, he could hide from everything, possibly even start fresh and tear away from the skin of history and that annoying, surveillant eye of the sun.

The night was darkness, though the sun was still having its tantrum across the edge of the sky. Frank was the dark cloud hauling him behind, a parasol of stormy weather, eclipse of inertia. He sheltered Peter from the probing and moralistic rays that could splash around into so many nooks and corners, find something, anything, make everything where there wasn't anything. Each kiss of Ivory's was like that as well: righting him, by plummeting him down into his own black hole. So when he reached and placed his hand on Frank's shoulder, he knew why, but couldn't quite say, and Frank looked at him with implicit suspicion, as if the occurring situation was strange to both.

The wheels screeched and the van rocked through some of the more treacherous curves uptown. Each time it was like a razor cutting more fat off Peter's head. He wondered for a moment how old he was, but when the number *twenty-seven* came to his head it seemed to bear no relation to him or his experience. Surely, the years stacked up, but they were nothing to be collected, were lone stars burning out on their own. Each had ruined him, devoured what was best in him, as they digested him like a sequence of unimaginably large worms. The city too. The city was influenza got up like a show girl, an ugly but seductive scar that had you lying in bed every night, holding onto your cock for dear life, exhausted out of your ever-jilted mind. In the city—in *The City*—no one wanted to know or be known, only to outdo and overdo the cold, psychotic roles they had come to establish. At this point, Peter was just about winning. He had finally learned the trick, and it was a lot simpler than he imagined it to be. It just took some time, and a little bit of effort—a bit of sticking-to—and all the distortion and confusion could be yours at such a small price. Little did he realize, months ago when he had begun making the drawings, with the distinct purpose of losing his grip on reality, that he'd find it so easy.

Several times Peter turned to Frank, gesturing, breathing as if about to say something, and then would stop.

"What?" Frank asked.

"I don't know. How long before we're out of the city?"

"That bridge we crossed five minutes ago took us out of Manhattan, and into the Bronx. If that's what you mean."

"Good." They weren't even out of the city, and Peter already felt like a different person. "Where are we going anyway?"

"I have some friends in different places." Frank was silent for a while, as if about to confess something. "What about you, any desires?"

Peter struggled with that question a moment. "Oh, you mean places to go? Let's see." He rubbed his chin and thought about the lines and names on the map, places he'd never gone, but was curious about. They curled and wound about in his mind. Newburgh, Peekskill, Walden, Kingston, New Paltz, Saugerties, Coxsackie, Dobbs Ferry, each detonating their own little circle on a black or red line that looked shakily drawn by someone frightened or overexcited. He jogged them around in his head for a while, repeating their sounds, and then fell asleep. When he awoke they were pulling into a rest station. Peter fidgeted, complaining of a full bladder.

"We should really go inside, anyway," Frank said. "These places offer a really interesting birds-eye view of . . . I think you'll see what I mean when we get in there."

Nearly everyone was wearing an athletic suit—enough brightly colored nylon to sail a whole fleet of racing yachts across the Atlantic—although most of them looked as though they hadn't moved a muscle in years. They lined up at stations in a fast food court with almost every imaginable brand name, many odd-shaped and cartoonish. These were the people left back on earth, picking their ways through their less adventurous lives, when the Starship Enterprise took off for other galaxies. Here they were gathered together in an off-road refuge, its appealing and cozy fabrication, airing like bedclothes out a window. When Peter gets home, he decides, he will make drawings of them, not of the individuals themselves, but of what he found to be their commonalties, and in that way attempt to release them from their servitude, a way of justifying his hooky-playing. Above, the wooden ceiling, peaked and blandly weathered much like those found in modern Protestant churches, as per the failed disciples of Frank Lloyd Wright, made Peter's heart feel as though it was shrinking and turning gray, making him think that these were people who had one foot, not in the grave, but in a synthetic toy dog-poop. "Where's the bathroom?" he asked Frank.

Peter went upstairs to the men's room and peed into a fragrantly scented urinal. He found his way back to the information desk where Frank had said they should meet. There were dozens of flyers advertising canoe trips, cavern tours, family resorts, all directed nostalgically at a world he had wanted, but could never believe existed; imagined memories of family outings, he and Sally getting fat and stupid, driving in their sweats to every brochured haven, repeating pattern after pattern on the map until they died. Now, it was true, he *could* die alone, but these were the people who had decided not to die alone, and what a cost. They learned a vocabulary of work and leisure, so that if someone dropped dead there would always be a replacement, while he opted for nothing, but without intent, as if some facet of his intelligence had gone undeveloped.

It was completely dark by the time they got back on the road and the highway was strung like Christmas lights. A red beacon was flashing up about a quarter of a mile. Several more appeared. The traffic was slowing until they inched along. Frank was rocking the van with the brakes every time he had to slow down. There was an odd pleasure in his face that Peter recognized but didn't want to think about. By the scene of the accident the traffic had all but come to a halt. A shiny red Pontiac had run up beneath a trailer and stood crushed and mangled like a beer can that had been hit by a lawn mower. The blood ran out of Peter's face and he felt thirsty. Within a corral of flares two bodies lay in black bags that flattened above the shoulders. Peter's curiosity forced his hands to shaking. How had they gotten the bodies out and why? Streaks of dark sheen spread across the pavement. He put his head back and closed his eyes trying to imagine he was back home, held in the arms of a supernal and hollow woman. But the accident confirmed something for him. There had seemed to be an emerging pattern in his life, like parallel entity of effect, and now he safely knew, though not for how long, or what it would cost him.

Frank suggested they make camp soon. This came as a surprise to Peter, who hadn't slept outdoors for some time, though he hadn't considered where else they might be spending the evening. And the fact that he hadn't been thinking about it also surprised him—he always worried about things like that: where he'd be sleeping, eating, shitting, whether or not he had the money to pay for any of the three or all, and what he had to do not to offend his host if he was getting it at no cost. He was wary, but didn't say a word because he didn't want to seem timid, or to be a bad sport. They would camp out. Peter trusted Frank enough to do that. After all, what could happen? Thousands of people do it every day. Millions of people do it every day, actually live that way, since they can't afford to build houses, and even if they could, someone would come along and blow it up sooner or later anyway. So Frank pulled off the thruway, without protests from Peter, who was anxious besides all common sense reason not to be. They got on a two lane interstate. There were only lights around the small towns they drove through, otherwise they could only see the road by the lights of the van, except around curves, where there were reflectors. After about a half-hour Frank turned down a side road that narrowed to nearly one lane wide. It seemed they were driving through a dark tunnel under the branches of trees. An occasional branch would screech the roof of the van like a claw.

Frank pulled into an unpaved drive with a rope hanging across it and a no trespassing sign. He stopped the van and asked Peter to loosen the one side so he could drive in. Peter wriggled in his seat. "Can't we get arrested for doing this?" he asked.

"You can get arrested for just about anything if somebody sees fit."

Peter got out, as requested, unhitched the rope, and then re-hitched it as Frank and the van passed through. The road was still muddy and well rutted from heavy rains the week before, with a gradient steep enough to give the engine a little trouble. Out the side window it was darker than Peter ever remembered seeing it, though out the front nearby, if not well-defined, objects were lit up brightly from the headlights, carving out a mobile clearing that welled out for yards ahead of them. The area around the road was thick with trees and undergrowth, vast snakes of vine casting out before them and disappearing into the verdure. Where the road got too steep to go any further Frank found a clearing under a huge foliated branch where he could hide the van. He told Peter to grab his things, and handed him a lantern, the rolled up tent, and a plastic jug he had filled with water, and set out ahead with a huge twelve-volt lamp up the muddy bank. Peter followed behind slipping up the hill in his boots, trying to walk sideways using the edges to grip deeper, making small platforms for each step.

They came to a shallow stream and turned off following it for about a hundred yards or so until they arrived at a depression in the slope about fifty feet wide. Frank hung his sack on a branch stub of one of two trees that grew out at an angle from one another, joined at the bottom by a seam where the two trunks kissed. The light wiggled for a moment and then searched the ground through winter-mulched leaves, dead branches, an occasional rock jutting out green like a shrunken hillside draped in shadows. There was already the sound of crickets in the air and a hoot now and then from some kind of night bird. They set their things down and Frank began feeling around with his foot for a spot even enough to sleep on. Peter watched awkwardly until Frank began taking wads of mulch and covering an area he had found. Peter joined him, like a child mimicking an adult until he was told there was enough.

Frank tossed Peter the tent, gave him the flashlight to work with and began clearing a spot for a fire. Peter spread the tent out and got the stakes in but had trouble getting the poles to stand up. He'd stand one and the other would fall over, and continued like this a few times before realizing that they needed to be tied down with the nylon lines hanging from the front and back. So he got out two of the four stakes he thought were extra and noted that there were two other lines hanging from canvas loops toward the middle of the tent. When he finally got it all worked out it stood firm enough, although slightly warped. He stood looking at it for a while and then went to help Frank kick around for small wood dry enough to add to the fire that Frank had started.

All the while, Peter was anxious. He never thought of himself afraid of the dark, but this dark was blindness, except where the outline of the trees met the sky above and where the trail of the flashlight fell. It was so dark he felt as if he had coal rubbed in his eyes, or that some unknown animal made of black air had landed on his face. It had its own inky life, and it wasn't very inviting. Whenever he had gone camping before it was with a larger group of people, and they had arrived during the day and had enough time to get a large fire set, and hung lanterns of all sorts in the trees. At worst you had to hide in the outer perimeter of light to pee. He was afraid of what was hidden away from the beam, and what the beam might reveal, all the while knowing it was completely irrational to have this fear, and panicking all the more for it. With care he bent over to feel the fallen branches for dampness, lifting them up and stacking them under one arm, while the trees they had fallen from towered maliciously above. He looked them over, muttering apologies under his breath. But it was in vain. The trees wanted no part of his scavenging, nor his words or well-wishing. If they could move, if they could force their limbs in whatever direction like animals could, they would swat at and crush him like a berry between their viney fingers.

After they had gotten the fire built up to the point where it was throwing a reasonable amount of heat, they sat, Peter on a large rock, and Frank on his bed roll with his legs crossed over a mat of leaves. Frank had taken out a bottle of Old Grand Dad bourbon that was wrapped inside his bedding and took a couple of swigs while he slouched gazing into the flames. When he handed it over, Peter extended his hand warily and held it up to his chest, resting his chin on the neck.

"Have a drink," Frank said, gesturing. "It's okay. Let's just not get piss drunk. That's all."

Peter lifted the label to his face. It was illuminated slightly from the fire light behind, just enough to make it out, a dark patch over the luminescent amber liquid, which caught his eye and seduced him with its warmth. He was anxious, although this is like the nights he often dreamed of having, the cool air on his back, the warmth on his chest and face, the quiet blackness all around. Yet he was haunted and he wished he was back home in some smoky bar, hovering over a pint, occasionally asking the bartender what music was playing on the tape. Dreaming about Sally. The changes rolling through his life left him feeling vulnerable. Anything could happen to him out here. He wondered if he should drink, whether he should let go and let whatever happens happen to him. He dared himself and took a long slug. And then another.

"There you go. Wait, slow down!" Frank said with a broad smile. "Save some for me." He took the bottle away and took another drink to catch up and then screwed the cap back on. "I know," he says standing up. "I'll be right back. I've got an idea."

Frank scampered away over a hill toward the van. While Peter was alone with the fire it seemed to be playing games with him. Now and then when he relaxed enough to loosen his stiff posture, letting himself drop forward, a tongue of flame would suddenly lick his way coming very close to his face and driving him back again. This happened several times and he sat upright more cautiously until in a hot blast the whole fire drove in his direction. He slid back on his rock a few inches, feeling his singed eyebrows, and noted how funny it was because the air seemed to be quite still. But when he turned his attention from the breathy roar and snapping of the fire he heard the leaves rustling, whispering like a dry sea of ash and bones.

A dark silhouette appeared against the sky over the hill, bringing with it a thin spiraling sound that doppled as a rectangular box swung from side to side. As it approached, Frank's image took light from the fire. He had brought back a tape player and explained that he had been experimenting alone in the studio with something no one else had yet heard. It was an appropriate time to share it with someone because of the mood of the evening, he said. He had layered several tracks of guitar, all distorted and at high volume. Nothing was done in any particular key, rather he played either concordantly or discordantly depending on what was already on the tape. It went from muddled gargling to sweet melodies, sometimes fugue-like, or a factory of demon-possessed machines gone off the rails. Frank left the box at a distance from them and left the volume on low so that the music blended with the other sounds.

Peter listened. *Really* listened—it drew him in—as if there were messages coded in the noise and intervals, the metallic stress marks cutting through the air to him. They sifted through his head, bringing torn fragments of stars, husks of pine needles, mulch dust, cobwebs orange with the sting of fire. But it was very quiet. More than churn, it whispered along micro-currents of air through the leaves of trees. While the fire whipped and snarled, and leaves hissed and chattered, another species of plant or crawling thing—not readily noticeable, but penetrating virally into the inner recesses, thronging fibers vibrating tenuously snapping, curling—wove in him a stupor, as the other figure sat limp and ape-like. Through the barking, crinkling shards of aluminum, curled tiny flames and robot hands reaching and dying. The fire stomped and leapt in time with the machine-shop rhythms. Peter felt like something was plucking wires attached to his teeth, grinding them to break free of the sensation. He turned and reached for the bottle from Frank, who sat upright again, extending his arm.

"You know," said Frank, as Peter took a long drink. "Eerie. It's eerie out tonight. That's good, because I want to tell you a story."

"I thought it was just me."

"It kind of reminds me of a night like this a couple of years ago. I was back in New York visiting a friend, and he dragged me out to someplace like this, I don't know, maybe a hundred miles northwest of here. I didn't really want to go. I had just spent a week or two out in the Sierras with no place to go but the wild. Part of my training. It was great, don't get me wrong, but you ache for a public watering hole after a while. So here I was back in New York, bars everywhere like trees in the forest, and Irv—his name was Irving—tells me he's got to bring me out into the country again so I can sit around a fire with some old college professor of his. This guy was supposedly half Algonquin and half something else I don't remember, and he'd learned all that medicine mumbo-jumbo from an uncle or something. He'd get into it now and then when you got him loosened up enough, sometimes, you know, just for entertainment, and I have to tell you, he really spun my head. I felt like I was tripping-out on some of the nasty weed one of the guys had, thought it was treated with DMT, or something. Then I explained it away by suggestion, hypnosis, or something like that, but everyone there assured me they saw and heard the same thing I did." He stopped and poked the fire with a stick.

"And?" said Peter.

"It was kind of a night like this."

"So, what happened?"

"All kinds of crazy shit. But I better stop now, 'cause you'll never believe me. And even if you could, you'd never get to sleep tonight."

It both made Peter mad and sent a trill of excitement through him. "You make it sound as though it would be a desirable capacity, you know, to be gullible."

"It would. In a sense. I think you've been through that with Alex already."

Peter rolled his eyes. He hated the way Frank could feign madness better than he could himself, after all the effort he had put into the project.

"Okay, I know what you mean, but tell me."

"Let's just say it was your favorite horror flick, the one that really makes you shit your pants, but one you are living moment to moment, with a bit of the sacred thrown in."

Peter felt a smirk of embarrassment cross his lips, despite his own most recent fugue states which posed in contradiction to his skepticism, his supposed *Bellamonia*. As he listened further, and his anger grew, he felt disturbed as well by the apparent distress with which Frank spoke. He wanted to stand up and walk away, throw something into the fire, or just punch Frank in the mouth, and found that he was wrestling with something bottomless, a seldom but determined tendency that spread throughout his body like an influenza once it got started. And the maggot wanted nothing more than to infect him with Frank's world, the one he seemed to dress himself within, as if out of a costume shop, with all its superstitious crappery hanging on like frills. It was an accomplice world that helped slip Peter further into the one he had begun to concoct since Horace died.

"I know this all sounds silly," Frank said with a grin.

"Not at all. Go on. Go on." Peter seethed, but held onto himself, knowing it would pass.

Frank laughed, hearing the seriousness in Peter's voice. "Don't worry about it. I'm kidding you. Well, not completely."

Frank looked straight at Peter with challenge in his expression and went on. "He did exorcisms on both of us that night. We both needed it." Peter's throat tightened as images flashed through his head. Something in him felt like prey in a cul de sac, that he had rounded the corner and was about to be consumed, to be devoured and burned from the inside out by some slow spreading poison within him. There had been warnings all along, a life advertised with the encroaching glare of the demonic, only now to be realized, and it was perhaps too late to save himself. After all he didn't believe in Jesus, or any of the other avatars of goodness and light. Who else could caste out devils? Another more powerful one that would only take its place? He was being eaten from the inside by a dark dampness that singed and smoked like a circuit overloaded, gone to the fritz. It was the only explanation, why everything was becoming so odd, warped in the mirror, why he was acting like someone he had never met, gone

193

rabid. Dread bored out a little hollow within him, and filled it with a noxious gas that would explode once the right kind of flame grazed it. It was a matter of time. If he wanted to, if he could find his will to pay attention to it he could count the seconds. One. Two. It would be the earnest thing to do. The more he ignored it, trying to go on as if nothing was wrong, the deeper it would grow, spoiling everyone else's chances around him. Frank and Ivory seemed invulnerable, somehow, seemed to thrive on it. They were being used. But then maybe they were his only hope for redemption. He was playing chess with something much smarter and better than him. All he could do is sit back, wait, watch.

"But it wasn't what you think." Frank continued poking at the fire with a stick, each jab releasing a rhythmical flair, a chanting of sparks that bypassed the brain but spoke directly to Peter's body.

He watched, his hands growing cold from the iciness that had moved in and taken control of his nerves and most of his attention. At the same time his head had grown so hot he thought it was burning, not from the fire, but from inside, where another fire burned, and he could smell the taste of an electric transformer overheating, like the one that burned out when he electrocuted himself with the toy trains when he was about three or four. The memory came back to him vividly, the first time the thing had gotten into him and made him jump and fried his hand to an aching soreness that lasted for days. Something in him was dead from that point forward, and the ghost of whatever it was had turned against him and all of life.

Could it be that his eyes were playing tricks on him, or were there people moving around in the trees? He couldn't hear them. The sound of the fire was drowning them out. But then maybe there was a voice, or was it the fire mutating through his nervous ears. They were shadows, had to be. But wait! That was a face, surely! Were they locals snooping around? Maybe they would call the police and they would have to leave the woods and get a room in town. That would be a relief.

In the shadows by the periphery of light stood Horace and a dog, but in his fright Peter opened his eyes realizing they had been closed, a rush of adrenaline bursting into his head. A close one. He didn't believe it, not really, but the chronic and obsessive notion that there was some sort of malign, nonphysical entity inhabiting him, warping his thoughts and perceptions, was playing in his back brain and erupting into his forebrain at rapid intervals. It didn't matter it was pure fantasy, that it was impossible. The impossible is always possible, as had been shown consistently throughout history, though in his own life the opposite always seemed to be the case. He sat tight thinking of all the imagined possessions and terminal illnesses he had suffered. *Illnesses of the imagination* only, perhaps, but what does that mean? What was it that persisted in making him fall to pieces as soon as he found himself in unfamiliar circumstances? In the spooky, nonscientific world of the forest, warmed by the chaotic insinuation of a bonfire, the distinction between possession and psychosis fell away, and he sat at the brink of that third indescribable thing, feeling how easy it would be to step into its snare, if only to satisfy some bored and adventitious part of him who still wants to rock out. Perhaps he should have himself an exorcism, he thought, just for the hell of it, see what happens. But wouldn't that just push him further, make him even more of a victim of his own machinations than he already was? Resist.

He tried being as scientific and common sensical as possible, but it was a desire born of panic that kept him slipping. All the laws, he got to thinking, had to come from somewhere, and if it was another intelligence, like his own, then *it* was surely up to no good, and was no doubt singling him out and provoking him for its own entertainment. Everything was light and mass. The light of the fire playing against the trees creating shadows. Everything was clear for a moment, but then not. Frank had disappeared, possibly off to sleep, leaving him alone with the fire and the things in the dark without an anchor. It wasn't what was around him so much that was the problem, but whatever it was that he was—a formless meandering within a tent of bones and flesh. Back again to his mind. And he mused for a moment about how all of human history could be seen as an attempt to chase the ghosts out of the forests. But they would gather around laughing, immutably, unshaken except by laughter. Either completely deny or spend your life getting chased around terrified. There were two kinds of people in the world and he couldn't figure out which he was. Which did he want to be? Denier or terrified? Neither. If only he could create a world of his very own that was safe, but full of adventure. He had the impulse to laugh at himself, but was frozen.

To this the fire answered him with a spank to the air. It wasn't one flame, but a composite of many flames, some lasting, some existing only for moments before dying and giving birth to something new. In this way it was like himself, countless selves joined in a dizzy juncture, fornicating and devouring one another in blind combustion. The limbs of dead trees lay beneath them. They were like his arms and legs riddled through with death spasms of light and intense heat, yet he was there, safe against his rock, the beneficiary, but unraveling, splitting and dying, and sputtering off into thousands of pieces. No thought could last more than a flickering instant, and then another and another, like blows on the head. If the flames were the ghosts of wood then he too would have a ghost. A chill went through him. His body was on fire and that was what sees and hears and feels and thinks. It was necessarily agonizing. He could almost speak to the flames before him. They were speaking to him, telling him this.

He sat like that for maybe hours, not remembering at what point Frank had disappeared or knowing what it was that stood him up and lead him down to sleep. He dreamed he stood outside the tent, face to face with a huge man made of fire. The man said nothing, just stared hotly and deeply into his eyes, so far down to a place he'd never reach on his own. He was a devil. Peter could tell by the menacing power that probed him effortlessly. But he wasn't there to harm him, just to be marked and terrify, and that he did. Peter flew out of the tent and then stood paralyzed with a numbness in his body as if his spine had been split. His mind was completely still because his brain was being broiled alive. When the heat became unbearable, pictures started rolling in his head, and he saw that the man of fire had black roots that went down into the ground, growing darker the deeper they plunged, until the fire was black, and hottest where it was blackest. Looking back at the man's feet he saw that they were also his own.

He shook himself out of his sleep paralysis and awoke drenched in sweat inside his sleeping bag, scrambling out of the tent in a panic, but was caught in the murky darkness like that in his dream, but much cooler. Little flames moved around within him, but they were silver, with furry tails. They were squirrels. He stood motionless aware of them moving around within him, where they had always lived. He was after all like a tree. He was recognized and accepted finally amongst the others.

14

The next day they spent either tromping around in the woods or sitting and staring off into a void from an outcropping of rock. Peter felt great, electric, wired into the whole root, leaf and stem panoply around him. He couldn't believe how much better he felt after just one night out of the city. His obsessions about Sally and Horace seemed left behind over the space they traveled. He felt unplugged from the machines and re-plugged into the vegetation and the prancing about of small animals, a sense of belonging he hadn't had for a long time. But toward later afternoon, with some mild protest, he let Frank talk him into saying good-bye to their campsite and loaded himself into the van.

It was a couple of hours drive to Saratoga, so they decided to pull off for a meal on their way. The day was just beginning to grow dark, and they had to soon decide whether they were going to camp again and risk the chance of rain, or get a room in a motel. By the time Peter was through with a greasy truck stop meat loaf he was feeling heavy and tired. Frank was in an easy enough mood to go along.

Most of the motels in town were booked, so they backtracked up the highway until they found a place whose entrance was almost blocked off entirely by road construction. They rode up the ramp and through the narrow drive, which lead to the parking lot. It was unpaved gravel, worn down to the dirt in some spots. The rooms were situated in two story row houses. The office was in a large mobile home that had become rooted to the ground over the years. A set of wooden steps led up to the doorway, and the two mounted them and were greeted by three large cats. Frank rang the buzzer on the wall adjacent to the door as Peter peeked through a window. A middle-aged couple sat at a table eating dinner. The TV was blaring. They could hear it from outside. The man, hearing the second buzz and the bark of the dog that had started as they had gone up the steps, staggered to his feet and walked to the door, disappearing from view of the window. When he reappeared it was in the open doorway. His mouth smiled, full of grayish brown teeth, filling the air with an odorous breath seasoned heavily with alcohol. He spoke with a spraying slur. His wife, also smiling, also inebriated, was turned around to face the two as they were invited in.

"Come in. Come on in!" he told them. There was a shifty look in his eyes that made Peter uncomfortable. He was met by the dog on the way through the door, and was almost knocked back out over the threshold, but he stepped to the side, nearly placing his foot in a litter box filled with enough shit to start a garden. They signed for the room, and paid with cash up front, twenty dollars each, no questions.

The room was small, with two twin beds with lumpy mattresses, and a big old black and white TV, probably over twenty-five years old. They were surprised it worked, although it did only barely. They pulled it out so it could be seen from the far bed, and they both laid down for a while and watched. Nothing much was on. The news. Some old re-runs of series neither of them had ever seen. On one channel were some Bugs Bunny cartoons, but they faded behind snow before long.

Around nine o'clock they decided it was time to go out. Frank told Peter about several bars he had hung around in when he had been touring with a band. They would surely still be there. Peter grabbed his coat from the rack, which took the place of a closet, and noticed a woman's shoe lying on top. It was a low healed dress shoe you'd expect an older woman to wear. Printed inside were the words "Morning Bird." It made Peter think of a huge aging woman flapping her arms and lifting spritely off into the air.

The first place they tried was jazzy and nostalgic, with frosted glass and a well-kept tin ceiling, but otherwise dull and featureless, except for a young woman in a shimmering blue dress who caught Peter's attention. He felt he recognized her from somewhere deep in his past. He couldn't keep his eyes off her, though she was obviously with the muscular fraternity fellow beside her. The next place was just as bad or worse, kind of a tavern grill that catered mostly to young couples in a rush to appear several years older. Down the block was *Tar and Feathers*, Frank recalled, one of his favorite spots, although likely not to get too lively since most of the students in the area were home on holiday. That was fine with Peter. He felt more secure with space around him.

The crowd seemed to be mainly local blue collar. A basketball game was playing on the television, people were playing pool. The juke box was playing *American Pie*. Peter had been standing by the doorway until Frank had finally pushed him in the back and directed him toward the bar. A bottle of Gennesee Cream Ale was placed in his hand and Frank asked him if he would like to play some pool since the table was free. But Peter was drawn over to the Shuffle Bowl game, having not seen one in years.

"We'll play that later," Frank said. "The table's open now. It won't be for very much longer."

Peter shrugged and lumbered over to the table, still a bit in a dream, images of the blue dress woman, Sally, Ivory, and dozens of other women flashing and coalescing in his head, unable to focus enough to feel committed. Frank put money into the coin slot and the balls went clattering down. Peter took a cue and stuck one end near his eye and looked down the edge to see if it was warped. He couldn't tell. They all looked straight to him no matter how bent they were, and they were all bent. It was something he felt, an intuition perhaps. He took it as a sign that gave further meaning to his experience the previous night, the warping of the wood the way it coiled when it burned – another part of a subtle information feed, from the unknowable place he was plugged into, somehow, receiving, giving, a sharing of data among branches of the ineffable machine made of everything.

Frank invited him to break and he almost missed the rack completely, slicing off three balls from the corner and loosening the rest only slightly.

"I can tell this is going to be an interesting game." Frank was expressionless, but his eyes moved around the table sniper-like, seeking a position. He went for a second break and sent the corner ball into the corner pocket, and then lined up three more in a row before handing the cue back to Peter, who knocked in an easy shot, but scratched.

The pattern continued more or less for the next three games and two beers. Peter was buying, since he was losing, waiting for the secret of the wood to emerge from the cue, showing him not only how to shoot, but how to be. A couple of locals came over, both with rounder and fuller bellies than even his own, brawnier arms too, and tanner, compared to his pale and fleshy tubers. The larger man was being called Chief, and indeed he was the spitting image of the Chief character from *One Flew Over the Cuckoo's Nest*. If Peter was a tree, he was a sapling, and this man was a mature oak, though he looked more like a lumber jack in his thermal and flannel shirts.

During the several rounds of doubles they played they came out about even, no thanks to Peter's playing. But this didn't bother him since he realized the mysteries of the wood had to come slowly. He was carefully watching the others as they played. The other man was hairy and energetic, and sweat soaked the underarms of his sleeveless tee shirt. His voice was loud and metallic, and though he seemed to be enjoying himself, moved with an impulsive violence, and brusque unsettling gestures. Peter hid deep within a sphere of torpid daze he had carried with him, of which the other was only surface chink.

He looked over at Frank, who was un-phased as always, and took the cue from Chief and aimed for another easy shot. He noticed that his hands were shaking, but held them still hoping no one had noticed. When he missed, the man in the tee shirt grinned, looked away, and yanked the cue from Peter's hand.

A man with a grey Fu Manchu and John Lennon glasses slapped a stack of quarters down next to Peter just as he was taking his next shot. It caused him to send the cue ball spinning off wildly but he was relieved that they wouldn't be playing another game for a while. His playing this last time around had assured that. When they were done he dug into his pocket for his remaining change and dragged Frank over to the Shuffle Bowl game in the corner, away from the others where they could disappear.

He was leaning on a counter beside Frank as he took his shots. His face twisted and folded up as he tried in earnest to dig in to retrieve some thought that would bring him back to a common place with the others around him. One would be there waiting for him sometimes, and he almost felt as if it was there now. It slipped around in his grasp and disappeared, then came back again almost long enough for him to see. But a hot repugnance in his chest swallowed it every time he thought he had it. He chased it until his mind was blank and giddy, a foamy mixture with his beer. Now and then it was interrupted by the game, where he would escape into moments of brief excitement, nothing remaining but the tightness in his throat.

When they were done playing Frank went back to the pool table to play with the townies and Peter sat down at the bar, playing with a swizzle stick and stared flatly at the men running and jumping around with a basketball on the TV. The score was irrelevant, as were the teams that were playing and the activity they were engaged in. It hardly mattered what color their uniforms were. It was a bored and meaningless stare that happened for the sake of his eyes and their need for distraction, as if they had themselves chosen what to do. If it wasn't that Chief had sat down next to him he would have numbed off almost into sleep.

Chief was half drunk, but was friendly enough when Peter asked him what other places were around. He was only going to be in town a day or two and he wanted to make the best of it, he said. Chief shrugged and said, "This is it." Peter shrugged back and tried to say something intelligible about the game, but Chief said he had already lost all his money.

Peter bought a round. Both tried making awkward conversation, a blind date between introverts with nothing in common. Peter was growing more and more frustrated and it appeared that his drinking partner was getting impatient with his cross-examinations. He tried one last time and risked offending him by asking him if he had heard of the college professor who did the Indian medicine show. Chief perked up. He knew right away the man Peter was referring to.

He laughed and said, "Yeah, the guy's a real crazy clown, but I tell you he can make it work sometimes. I wouldn't go near him with a fifty-foot pole, though. I think he's playing around. Not good. My grandfather used to work some of it himself. He was also crazy, but a little more serious. Still, he used to scare the shit out of me when I was a kid. The guy you're talking about, I think he lost his job at the university because he was involving the students too much in his fun and games. Not his place. He didn't know everything. Medicine, they call it, but sometimes he'd cause more problems. I think he opened a pizza joint. I heard it's the only pizza place that looks more like Mexican. I never looked for it. I wouldn't want to know what he put in the sauce. Mostly, he's a phony with a few tricks."

Peter suspected he knew more, but Chief was evasive.

"Back in the city where you're from... I suppose that's where you're from. You smell like the air. I go there to work sometimes and when I come back I smell for a week. I drink to sweat it out, but then I smell of that too." He laughed heartily and then turned back to Peter with drunken, soulful eyes. "Where you come from there are many types of medicine. You have some from Africa and Haiti, stuff from China and all that, but none of them cats especially want to be your best friend, you know, because of the way you white folk get sometimes, if you know what I mean." He laughed again, this time looking back, grinning a little more maliciously. "And even some Indians teaching that adult education crap. But you know, you're a drinker like me, and I think it doesn't pertain to you." Chief grinned again with challenging penetration that put Peter off balance.

"I was just being curious, that's all. I didn't mean anything by asking you, really."

"That's alright. I know when you see an Indian you probably make the mistake of seeing the souvenir shop Indian, which is little better than the kind that gets shot at by cowboys on TV, and because you don't know us as people you make judgments by hearsay. You see either a drunk or a witch doctor, but to tell you the truth we are what we are, and sometimes that's both, and perhaps if you're more sophisticated you might go a little beyond that into that confused muddle of all the things we are, but that will never be far enough. And that's the same with you. You don't know what it means to be like me, and most of the time it means nothing at all except having to work a lot of shitty jobs and live in a way you don't think is right. That's all."

He stopped for a moment to think and take a drink from his beer.

"It just so happens that I do know whom you're talking about because not many of us get to work at the university, and even fewer of us get to exploit what we know about our history, because it's all your books we have to teach. Now, some of us might because he's a wise guy, and he's half caucasian and he's considered a clever fucker and an artist."

By this point Peter was ready for the conversation to end. He didn't want to argue about whether or not his interests were authentic or simply a fashion statement, or whether he had a right to say anything at all about the experience of general human suffering. Whatever expectations he had about the man had been turning into instruments of self-loathing since they began, something like the foolishness he felt when he had been making his first few quests with girls during his school days. He felt hollow and insubstantial, a balloon of skin inflated with shame and self-ridicule. They were familiar up over a collapsing core, an anus sucking indefinitely empty and giving way under the *competing-enough*, the moments frequent as red cards in a playing deck. Innumerable layers of himself would fold demands of gravity and entropy. And it was a kind of *bad* he felt without reason, or perhaps from the food he had eaten on the road, or from some tic fever he had picked up in the woods, but there was no sweat and no vomiting, not yet. He tried to wade back towards calm stupefaction, but felt it shrinking down into the pit of his stomach, and as he sunk after it there was a remorseful coagulation of his many thoughts into a single heavy bead, and the memories of Sally and Horace rose to the surface. He imagined them one body, crouched before him as he rammed it in from behind his head, both voices striking from the one mouth, with a sound that could have come from the heads of Cerberus. Chief must be the man that Frank was talking about. He could see through him, and now he was punishing him.

Chief was oblivious to Peter's meltdown, and continued talking along various byways, still holding vaguely to his point. "Now, I've noticed over the past few years that the black man has made his prayers into kind of a boxing match. You can imagine them shouting at themselves in the mirror, rubbing their fists and learning how to talk loud so they don't even need a microphone to compete with the noise on the street. That could be made into real medicine. It has been made into real medicine. Just do what they do and you'll have power. And I noticed when I was working down in the city this past November that some of the kids were wearing ski clothes, and you would think at first that it was some sort of envy of the white man, but it wasn't. It's the new tribal dress for the space age. My people, for the most part, stay behind in their old ways, or just get mixed up in your world until they don't know who's there anymore. But the African descendent is the great inventor, and he'll be taking over the world again eventually. For better or worse. My money is for the far better, take it or leave it.

"But to tell you the truth, we are all the same medicine man, and so I am the person you came asking about, but not the way you think, because the story is really about a number of men and women, and somehow they all got attached to this one particular college professor who may or may not really exist, not in the terms you usually think about. The stories you hear may have originated with a college professor, or his mother, or cousin, or maybe even someone like me, but they converge around a single imaginary identity that is no more real than the stories you tell about your own personal history, or what you think of the people you think you know, or even me. You see a man you think of as a drunk, but in fact, I am only a casual drinker, and have played the role for you so I can then turn around like I'm doing here and break the chain in your expectation, that gaze of knowing you have about everything you come in contact with. I say this because you seem like someone who's recently seen himself, and that's kind of a rare thing, and it tends to not make us happy but we might end up being afraid. Consider this your exorcism, since all the demons in the world are the ones you create inside your head, but they play out in the world as if they were something real. And they are. Because they are you, they have made you, and you are the angel and the beast from the religion that haunts you, one from a desert people thousands of years ago, that permeates even the ketchup on the grocery shelf, this very beer we're drinking. None of it has any right to exist, no more than we do, all this your people coming to our home and destroying it, but in doing so laying the foundations so that both you and I exist, take form, be our own monsters and piss demons into the living, breathing pool of everything around you. Yes, this is your exorcism, but so was that jukebox song you heard just minutes ago, and shouty rap songs of the African descendent you hear in the street on the way home from work, or when a car pulls up with those loud speakers throbbing the bass through your teeth. Yes, I spend enough time in the city to know. We may have passed each other on the sidewalk, in the grocery, you buying beer and me a can of beans after long hours on steel girders. You are the demon, because you are possessed by everything you encounter, the machine you type your name and password into in the morning that keeps your bank account full, so you don't have to think about where to get your next meal, same job for years, working for the same confused rats, in the same fluctuating rat maze, that they built, that heaven built, your heaven, which is full of devils to people like me, to my people, who existed long before your ideas and people were even a thought, before your ice ages and mainframe computers, wearing the skins of animals, or perhaps nothing at all, and here we are sharing a beer because of a chance encounter. You think. But who knows if this was something by design? You and I here because someone or something brought us together, which is always the way things happen, because the world brought us together, and that's who we are. You, the hate machine, and me the wooden Indian selling cigars, because in your mind that's what your

TV had driven into your head, so there's no way for you to see the real world, and we are drunk on the not-knowing our senses keep us trapped within, with our memories enfolding over and over like a carpet rolled over itself a thousand times and made into a window you try to look through. I promise I have not put poison in your beer, but soon you will feel it, and you will hate me for it maybe but someday maybe not. Now go do what you have to do."

Peter was hardly listening, but enough had come through the periphery of his awareness to blend with the panorama. What he really wanted, he thought, was to stand naked upon a cliff in the interior of Africa, blowing sweetly on a reed flute. He would cover his skin with a mixture of fat, mud, and animal excrement to protect it from the sharp scalpel of the sun, and when it dried black and blistering like parchment it would begin to peal, and turn to dust, leaving beneath it his new brown skin, shining in the sun, invisible in the night. His feet would be quick and sure, his eyes would see in the dark. Never again would he ever be afraid of anything. That is why he preferred dark beer to light, and why her preferred brown liquor to gin and vodka. He was making himself into the next new species of god-like marsupials, skipping countless generations on the evolutionary tree, in a cross fertilization of his own genes.

He tried to explain this to Chief in a variety of broken sentences, but without luck. The man grew silent and wore a vinegary expression as if outwitted at some game of bluff. The further Peter pressed the man the more he receded into a granite silence until Peter realized that he had lost him completely. At which point Peter began to feel the impingement of the surrounding space. The jukebox music and the clinking and clattering of glass got closer, nearly pressing against his skin, and the bodies moving to and fro formed shadows on a screen around him just beyond his arm's reach. It was getting harder for him to breathe, although the shift back to the mountainside would ease this momentarily, but flickered and passed leaving him stranded once again. He got up from his seat, hoping to entice Frank into leaving. But when he did he caught his foot in the runner of the stool, bringing it down with him to the floor with a loud bang. This in itself was nothing, but for the fact that before he had hit the floor he had grabbed for the only thing within his reach, which just happened to be the huge back of the man with the sleeveless tee shirt. Peter had brought him down in the midst of lining up a shot, in a rough football style tackle, forcing the cue stick under the felt where it separated like a three-foot zipper, and driving the man's chin down against the edge of the table. When Peter began to stand up the man was still rolling on the ground holding his face and moaning. He grabbed him by the arm to help him up while Frank shouted for him to run for it. Peter looked up. That's when the first fist hit him on the side of the face, throwing him back against the bar, his neck turning on its hinge.

He felt a sharp pain on the side of his skull, then one on its back, and heard a squawk fly out of him he could barely identify as his. He attempted to stand up and opened his eyes a fragment of a second before he was hit again, the huge fist disappearing in a flash of blue light, punching a lapse in his consciousness that made his knees buckle and his arms drop to his sides like wet dish rags. He opened his eyes again, pulling himself up against the bar for support, watching indifferently as Frank tried to break loose from two men who were holding him back, watched as his face disappeared again behind the wide girth of forearm revolving back on the body's axis to be released again, this time in the center of his chest. His rib cage seemed to instantaneously swallow the man's hand and return it in a motion that felt as though it was designed to burst his heart like a balloon. Air sucked noisily into his throat through the wide circle in his mouth. Greenish snow flickered on the periphery of his vision. More shots came at his body now quicker but with less impact. Beneath them, starting deep down in the center of his torso, a rumbling began to rise and make its way to the surface. It seemed to be protecting him from further damage. He was okay as long as he didn't resist, in fact now there was little pain at all. It was the squirrels running through the tunnels within his body. They were moving so fast he could hardly tell what they were, but he knew.

It seemed like hours compressed into fractions of seconds when the man finally backed away out of breath, and Peter stood up and laid on his back across the ravaged pool table. It was there that the rumbling slowed and finally came to a stop. Frank, who had finally pulled away from the four arms that had clung to him, turned and sneered at his restrainers and bolted over to where Peter was lying. "Holy fuck! You okay?"

"Yeah." Peter's eyes scanned the ceiling, the white-painted tin tiles coated with dust and oily crud. "Just give me a minute.

213

I'm putting it back together. The seams need reupholstering."
He pointed upward toward no specific point, though there
was a focus coming through the glaze of his expression.

He raised his hand towards Frank and was helped upright,
rolling over to the edge of the table and up over the bumper.
Pain spread topographically through his body in segments
that seemed held together by a very thin tissue. Between
himself and his biology lay a fissure wide enough for him
not to mind. He was concerned for this thing that was like
a laboratory-animated corpse connected to him by some
mysterious power. But not too concerned. It had endurance.
He could feel it. Enough to get back to the city in one piece if
that's what he intended to do. Just what he intended to do was
quite up in the air at this point. He had now had the experience
he had come for. The knowledge had been bequeathed him.
If the man who had struck him had not been the master, then
it was the master who had been working through him. It was
time to move on now. No semblance of reality remained from
the day before. He had been pushed and he had leapt to a
new level of understanding. The influx of information was
pouring into him from somewhere between two of his lower
vertebrae. It flowed up his spine like a cheap gin and sugar
mixture, and when it reached his skull, made pictures come,
like a prerecorded lesson volume shot directly into his brain.
The images were moving very quickly but he understood
them all on some level, although he had no idea how to use
them. The time would come when there would be revelation
upon revelation, and they would weave their way into the
world around him.

Frank had helped Peter into the back of the van where he laid on an open sleeping bag. He then started the ignition and ran back into the bar with an aluminum baseball bat. It occurred to Peter that he hadn't thought about work at all over the past couple of days, and that was different for him. There would always be some worry about something left undone, or somebody he owed a favor to. Always the worry of whom or what he was ignoring now. For once, his own need was much more urgent, whatever it was. Not quite the need to escape, although in an immediate sense that's what it appeared to be. He had to get Sally out of his mind, that was true, but more than that there was a sense of mission, something unfolding he didn't yet comprehend. He laid still and the pain pulsed orbitally at points one after another. He was made fidgety by it, but tried to lie quietly and let the hurt have its due, knowing that if he did, it would leave him alone in time. His life was in another's hands and it, whatever it was, knew better than he what was in store and what his needs were. It was a dark thing, sinister even, but he knew he could do nothing but give in, wondering how he would be obligated.

Yeah, back at work—it was Saturday though, wasn't it—back at work he'd be hiding in his cubicle feeling guilty about letting his attention stray. Suspecting eyes would hover around trying to catch him at a moment when his were glazed by some faraway pleasure, to strike it in a maniacal accounting sheet located in a cerebral space where it could larva and morph into something much worse. Yes, paranoia was a core value of work. Peter knew that a spy needs alcohol, and the hope that he could hold his own when he went shot for shot with the boss. It was the only way. He could never go back to purely working again. But none of that mattered now. He was temporarily suspended in a free zone, without even knowing why or how. It had something to do with being unprepared for everything that was happening. Somehow a gate had swung open, possibly by accident. It swung open that night he embraced Ivory. It occurred to him that there must be something unique about him, otherwise he'd never known. Not a uniqueness one could brag about, it was like being double-jointed, or having a sixth toe on one foot.

Frank seemed to be away for quite some time, but when he returned he flew into the front seat and threw the van in drive, screeching the tires as a hard thud came from outside. Peter's eyes flashed open for a moment, then squinted while the vehicle wagged and undulated over a sharp drop and then fish tailed out into the street. The light darkened so that Peter could see very little. Frank had taken to the side streets. Peter could see the outline of the trees against the night sky. Then came the intermittent lights flickering. They traveled for a few minutes at an easy pace and swerved up a hill, halting on a bed of gravel at the motel. Frank got out of the van and shut the door. The side door slid open and Frank's silhouette slouched illuminated from behind by a vacancy sign. He didn't say a thing until after he shook Peter's foot.

"How you doing soldier?" he said as he leaned inside.

"Okay. Did you give the bat to that guy?"

"Yeah. I gave it to him all right, but I'm afraid we won't be able to stick around town. Those guys'll never find us here tonight, but they'll be looking for us tomorrow. Just remember never to come back here again."

Frank helped him out of the back. He was already feeling better. The fire squirrels were already well on their way to rebuilding him. Their flames were scouring him from head to toe with a pleasant sourness that broke into colors when they reached his head, pouring out of the fissure in the rear left side of his skull. The whole thing felt cracked, as if it had been made that way so that his brain could grow larger and contain the sap of information that was flowing into it. An arm slipped around his back and under an armpit, and the weight on his legs grew noticeably lighter. He couldn't believe how strong Frank was for his lankiness. The same thing must have happened to him at one time. He must know what's going on. That made Peter feel more secure. He had been learning to trust him more and more.

The room was oven-hot when they returned. Despite the week of balmy weather, the owner had neglected to turn the boiler down and the radiator and pipes were sizzling. Frank worked his way around, cranking the windows as far as they would open, and cracking the door open a half-inch. They left the lamps off, but put the TV on without sound to illuminate the space enough to navigate. The light flashed, swelled and shrunk, repeatedly in no discernible pattern, and the room took on an old horror flick ambiance that transformed their ambiguous sense of peril into an anxious curio. Peter's body seemed held together by stitches of pain that cycled him like a night train over sordid and rickety tracks. This blessed thing that was happening to him was not without its ghoulish qualities. The angels were monstrous surgeons when it came down to it, although they did beautiful work. It progressed with all the special effects he had come to expect, the oozing saps and crinkling bone and cartilage. If he could have seen it at an earlier part of his life, before his illustrative transformation, he would have been deeply frightened of himself. There were secrets that needed to be kept, some that most would never grasp, never desire or possibly understand knowing. It was the sacred spy lore.

Frank, of course, was in the know, in the knowing and understanding knowing, but the silent knowing was something Peter could not breach, was part of the contract. Never let any of them think he couldn't contain the information or it might be taken from him, a grave responsibility, being a spy, psychic spy in a complex world he had never imagined, and now he saw with the clarity of an anatomist, now that his training was over and he had to find his path, find something to do with it. This would occupy his mind for the rest of the trip, the whole meaning of it from the beginning. To get out of his rote circumstances, access what had ripened in him in a good environment to think, would restructure his thinking in a way that modified seeing.

He would have to get back to work somehow on Monday, and by then his clarity will have swelled to an animal devouring all of the dichotomy of work and play, leaving their bones behind in the shadow of his true labor. He knew it would have had something to do with his work, his place and context of working, now seeing that the evil he had done for years was not an evil of the first degree, but one of the unknowing of the actual nature of his crime which was nothing, now that he saw that his work was nothing. It was a mere scratching and wincing at the shadows of what his knowledge could not let him swallow, but only mildly choke on. The quiet infiltration was just beginning. There was no way of knowing the *who* or *what* he was spying on and spying for, only the faith that they or it could tap his mind whenever needed—a one-way connection.

Peter awoke sometime deep into the night, to a much hotter than even previous heat, and from this he reasoned, the hotel owner must be a hostile party, somehow opposed to their objectives, to Peter's growth as a being, and hence to his very survival. The devil was trying to boil them out, scurry them so they couldn't make their move. He sat tight and lay awake for hours, his thoughts loosening from the syntax that made it impossible to conceive anything beyond the minuscule box step and chatter of the arbitrary ordinary. Now and then came crunching and crackling sounds, the room collapsing or expanding, as if learning how to breathe with difficulty.

The difference in temperature may have meant they had carried him off to a different room, perhaps even a different region of the earth, with different weather. But if they had, then Frank must have gone with him. It looked like Frank, the way he looks when he's sleeping. His head straight back, his body to the side, one knee jutting out over the other. The first fissures of the ceiling were forming over him, creases from the in and out breaths that had slowly crept unnoticeably over the decades, finally coming to bear. Peter let out a long careful beam of words from his forehead, the ones who had surrendered and were no longer needed, knowing they would mend the plaster long enough for them to get out, but not much longer. He lay in it, the quietly conceiving flatus of sound shapes and their belated significance, sending the images upward to seal the schisms and perforations between the fragments.

They would have enough time to get breakfast and come back, but it would be risky. Better to go all at once, instead of leaving behind streamers to collect later in the dust. A good spy leaves nothing behind but scraps to lead his animal into a snare. Who was his animal then? The motel keeper. They would leave and he'd be buried under the heap of rubbish, asphyxiated by the whitewashed and historical paneling that tore down around him. It had an ego made of platinum, he could tell, but it was deadly. Deadly as any blood-sucking squirrel let loose in a garage full of rat snakes. Like a sermon of the demon father breaking cinder blocks with his knuckles as parishioners look on celibate, their button eyes falling out by the threads in headstone. Scratching his scrotum with five squirting fingers firing off rounds one by one and all together. Sealing his eyes shut, slowly cooking his blood and bones into erasure marks in the air, in which he lay hovering. Vanishing still, the mud boiling up around him. Silence.

Until the earthquake. Attached to Frank's hand and arm. Stood over his bed. A face the moon over the hillside of his hip.

"Come on, we've got to get out of here. There are plenty more things to see."

He knew. Peter knew for sure that Frank knew everything and didn't have to speak.

Groups of trees seemed to cling together by barely visible phosphorescence, placing a striated depth over the approaching foliage. Vines and roots of memories chucked up in his brain, spitting earth and dark husks of rotted leaves into the blue air like an overexcited dog striving to uncover some newly buried corpse. Peter held onto the dashboard above the glove compartment, his forearms nearly buckled in enthusiasm. As the van lurched ahead the road sang wheezing, occasionally firing angry tics out to the departing roadside. Frank sat straight and true, wedged into his seat like a grasshopper pinned to a peg board through the side. Only his arms moved, rotating the wheel minutely in little jerks like nerve spasms. As the sun broke through an eastern cloudbank, white heat settled on Peter melting him to a soft taffy, and he began to stick to the seat.

The smoke poured out of his head, and out of his limbs. It had been there forever, but now it was darkening his whole self, and the work was nearly complete. He was black as anyone had ever been, anyone who had survived the fire. He was bursting with so much light he was speechless, and couldn't think of a single thing to say that would make anything better or worse. He looked over at Frank, who looked back at him twice quickly, and almost seemed to shudder.

"You look bad, man," he said. "We need to get you back. Back to your rock goddess, and maybe some chicken soup. You need some love."

"I *am* love, mother fucker."

JOHN SCHERTZER lives in Brooklyn, NY, with his wife and fellow poet, Kathleen E Krause, their evil genius sons, Liam and Declan, and their dog Rex. His poetry, fictions and hybrid pieces have appeared in a number of journals, including Big Other, Inverted Syntax, Danse Macabre, The Germ, American Letters & Commentary, LIT, Shampoo Poetry and others. He has taught poetry workshops at The New School in New York City, and edited the criticism section of 2 issues of LIT.